STAYING ALIVE . . .

"How well did he make the change from scholar to warrior?" asked Blade.

"Not as well as—" He broke off and shot a hard look at Blade.

Blade sensed that the instructor's suspicions might be aroused if he pushed any farther. But he also sensed he might be on the brink of learning something important. So he gambled. "You're a strange one to call a warlord 'young'," Blade said. "Unless he's hardly more than a child—you can't be much more than—"

"I'm ten times older than he is in what counts now! He's thirty, but he didn't [illegible] sword at six, or kill [illegible] [illegible]ght in pitched b[illegible] [illegible]gh it! And he di[illegible] [illegible]en—I did!"

Blade dropp[illegible] [illegible] push it. Certainly [illegible] point of provoking the instructor to a fight. Blade learned enough to know that he would have to be careful. His eyes would have to be looking in all directions at once, his hand ready to snatch up a spear, and his feet ready as a cat's to jump. It was the only way of staying alive in Dimension X . . .

The Blade Series:

#1 THE BRONZE AXE
#2 THE JADE WARRIOR
#3 JEWEL OF THARN
#4 SLAVE OF SARMA
#5 LIBERATOR OF JEDD
#6 MONSTER OF THE MAZE
#7 PEARL OF PATMOS
#8 UNDYING WORLD
#9 KINGDOM OF ROYTH
#10 ICE DRAGON
#11 DIMENSION OF DREAMS
#12 KING OF ZUNGA
#13 THE GOLDEN STEED
#14 THE TEMPLES OF AYOCAN
#15 THE TOWERS OF MELNON
#16 THE CRYSTAL SEAS
#17 THE MOUNTAINS OF BREGA
#18 WARLORDS OF GAIKON

PINNACLE BOOKS • NEW YORK CITY

This is a work of fiction. All the characters and events portrayed in this book are fictional, and any resemblance to real people or incidents is purely coincidental.

BLADE: WARLORDS OF GAIKON

An original Pinnacle Books edition, published for the first time anywhere.

ISBN: 0-523-00822-8

Cover illustration by Tran Mawecke

First printing, March 1976

Printed in the United States of America

PINNACLE BOOKS, INC.
275 Madison Avenue
New York, N.Y. 10016

WARLORDS OF GAIKON

1

Richard Blade was in his London flat. It was late evening, but he was not alone. The company was the kind he preferred at that time of night—or at any other time of the day or night when he was at leisure. She called herself Suzanne Aulin—a name that Blade knew was not her real one.

But her long brown hair was real and deliciously silky as he stroked it. Her clear complexion was real, and so were the long, dark brown lashes above very wide and bright dark eyes. Blade couldn't be sure if her figure was all real, because so far she was still fully clothed. But the curves under the red and green pantsuit were promising.

He ran a hand over the crown of "Suzanne's" head, stroking and caressing the fine hair, then down onto the back of her neck. He stroked the fine short hairs there, then brought his hand around and stroked the side of her neck. A receptive glow appeared in her eyes, and a very small, pink tongue crept out to moisten half-parted lips. His hand moved down, under the collar of her blouse, and felt the delicate ridge of her collarbone under the satiny skin. She moved closer to Blade on the sofa.

Blade took encouragement from that. Not that he ever really needed encouragement to approach an attractive woman—he was a man who lived life to the fullest and savored every moment of it, the dangerous ones as well as the tender or passionate ones. Blade considered for a moment what "Suzanne" might think of some of the things the man beside her had faced, some of the things he had done.

He was almost amused at the thought. Of course neither "Suzanne" nor any other woman he met would ever know about his far-flung adventures. The Official Secrets Act saw to that. He doubted if they would be amused even if they could know. Horrified, more likely.

Blade turned his attention back to the girl, who was now staring at him with aroused curiosity—and also aroused desire. His hands stroked her throat and neck again, then moved down to unbutton her blouse in a few swift motions. Under the blouse was nothing except "Suzanne"—she wore no bra.

She didn't really need one, either. The bare breasts that Blade could feel under his hands seemed full enough, subtly but beautifully curved, and as firm as perfectly ripened fruit. They were very real. Blade pushed the opened blouse and the leather vest aside and off the girl's shoulders. She lay back on the sofa, bare to the waist, as Blade ran his hands from her throat down to her navel. He followed his hands with his lips, nibbling and licking gently in the little hollow of her throat. He flicked the small, dark nipples with a fast-moving tongue until they stood up, swollen and engorged. "Suzanne" whimpered from deep in her throat, twisted her head from side to side, and thrust her pelvis up toward Blade.

Her nipples weren't the only thing around that was swollen now. Blade stood up to pull off his own shirt, then returned to the girl. His tongue explored her navel and occasionally wandered up to her breasts again. Meanwhile his hands worked slowly on the belt of her slacks. There was an urgency swelling in Blade's groin that made him want to rip off the girl's slacks and his own trousers and fall on her in an erotic fury. But he also wanted to slowly and teasingly build up her passion until it was as ready as his own to explode.

So he unbuckled her slacks and then drew them and the panties under them down over her hips and down her thighs an inch at a time. An almost invisible bulge at the base of her stomach came into view, then curls of dark brown hair. The smooth skin of her thighs had a pearly sheen in the dim light.

Now she was bare above the knees. A quick jerk, and she sprawled nude on the sofa. She looked up at him, smiling. Then her smile broadened as Blade rested one hand lightly on the curly, dark brown triangle exposed between her legs. With the other hand he began undoing his own trousers. If he didn't get them off now, he knew he would find it hard to get them off at all.

A moment later Blade was naked and standing up—and erect. "Suzanne's" eyes focused on his jutting maleness. His hand returned to the place between her legs, found the hair already damp, and probed deeply into a warm, wet cleft. She smiled. So did he.

"Petunia Bupp," he said softly, almost caressingly. He had ferreted out her real name before he had invited her up here for the evening. "Petunia Bupp. What an awful name for such a lovely girl. How—"

He felt her stiffen under his hands. Her eyes were still on him, but the passion had gone out of them in a split-second. Her mouth snapped shut so hard he heard her teeth click, and her lips tightened into a thin line. Her nostrils wrinkled as she took in a long breath.

Then the breath came out in a rush of words. "How—how the bloody *hell* did you find out my real name? It wasn't any of your damned business, you snoopy bastard! Why did you go looking for it? Why, damn you?"

She rolled off the sofa and snatched at her panties and slacks. Blade reached out for her, but she slapped his hand away. She stood up, balancing precariously on one leg while she tried to get the other into her slacks, glaring at Blade.

Her face was flushed—but not with passion—and her voice was almost shaking with shame and fury as she spoke. "You stupid, rotten—! You didn't think I might've changed my name for some good reason, did you? Well, it *is* an awful name. I hated it. I still hate it. Nobody's called me "Petunia" in three years. I thought I'd never hear it again. Now you looked it up like some damned spy, and you've spoiled everything!"

Blade found his voice. "Suzanne, I'm sorry. You—"

"Oh, never mind your being sorry!" she snapped. "You opened your big, fat mouth and that was it. I'm leaving. I can't stay here and make love to you, not after this. Not for a million pounds! I—oh, what's the use!" She sounded on the edge of tears. Blade stepped forward, arms outstretched to hold her, pull her against his chest, comfort and calm her.

Petunia lashed out with both hands. It was a hard blow but a clumsy one. Blade was an expert at several kinds of unarmed combat and normally it would have troubled him no more than a mosquito bite. But he was off balance and surprised. He sprawled backwards onto the sofa. Petunia snatched up her blouse and vest with one hand and her purse with the other and dashed for the door. As Blade struggled to his feet she vanished out into the hall, still bare to the waist. The door slammed behind her with a crash that made the glasses on the bar rattle and the cocktail forks jump off the coffee table onto the rug.

Blade swore. Not a placid man at the best of times, he was now filled with anger and frustration. He was tempted to launch a kick at the coffee table, but just in time he remembered that it was solid teak, four inches thick, with a marble top. The last time he had kicked it, he had spent the next week with three toes on his right foot in splints and bandages.

The memory cleared his head and made him laugh just as loudly as he had cursed. Poor Petunia. Poor, sensitive Petunia! He had had no way of knowing that she would fly into such a rage at the mention of her real name. Particularly in the middle of another sort of passion. But perhaps he should have guessed it and kept his mouth shut about the results of his little bit of research.

Yes, he should have. He had been a spy, in fact, and it was very much in his blood to go on being one whenever the chance arose. But like the American CIA, he had played spy in the wrong place at the wrong time.

Fortunately, he knew Petunia's address. He could and would send her a note of apology and perhaps some flowers and a bottle of her favorite sherry. That might get things back on the track again. But if not—well, the world was full of more women who would be good company than Blade would ever have a chance to meet if he lived to be a thousand years old.

Which, considering his profession, was bloody unlikely.

He crossed the room to the bar, opened it, and pulled out a bottle of Glenlivet and a glass. He had just put his hand on the soda-water siphon when the telephone rang. Blade picked up the receiver while he poured out the whiskey with the other hand.

"Hello, Richard?"

Blade couldn't help tensing for a moment, and he felt his heartbeat speed up in a brief flurry. The voice on the line belonged to the man called J. He was Blade's chief—among other things.

"Yes, sir?"

"Are you alone?" J had never approved of Blade's open and energetic pursuit of women, but he had never done anything to interfere with it, either. He would not do that to Blade, whom he loved like the son he had never had. Besides, it was simply not proper for one gentleman to intrude into the private affairs of another or to pass judgment on them. And J was a gentleman to his fingertips.

He was also one of the most formidable spymasters in the history of intelligence operations.

"Yes, sir." Blade couldn't help adding ruefully, "I hadn't planned to be, but that's the way it worked out."

J's voice held a tinge of amusement as he continued. "Well, then, Richard. Will you be free to be at the Tower tomorrow at eleven?"

Blade grinned. "Of course, sir."

"Very good, Richard," said J. "His lordship will be waiting." A click, and the line went dead.

Blade slowly put the receiver back in its cradle and finished preparing the Scotch and soda. Then he stretched out on the sofa and sipped it leisurely, savoring the smell and taste of every drop. It might be a long time before he tasted good Scotch again. In fact, he might never do so at all.

There was only one thing Richard Blade ever did at the Tower of London. He descended two hundred feet below it to a secret laboratory complex, to be strapped into a chair in the heart of a gigantic computer, the most advanced in the world. Then "his lordship"—Lord Leighton, England's most brilliant scientist—pulled a red switch. And Richard Blade vanished from England, to reappear—somewhere else.

That "somewhere else" they called Dimension X.

They would go on calling it Dimension X until they knew more about it, which would be a very long time. But Richard Blade was definitely the farthest-traveling man in the world, because he had been into Dimension X time after time. Each time so far he had returned to England alive and sane. Every journey into Dimension X was a grim battle for survival, and sooner or later he was going to lose one of those battles.

But Richard Blade believed that he owed England his best, everything his superb mind and body together could give. He had believed that when he was one of J's best agents in the secret intelligence agency MI6. He had gone on believing it when he became the only man in the world to travel into Dimension X and return safely.

2

Richard Blade was walking along the main corridor of the Project Dimension X complex below the Tower of London. J was walking beside him. The corridor stretched on ahead of the two men, apparently deserted and lifeless, with no ears to hear or eyes to see anything the two men might do. But Blade knew that every step he took, every word he spoke, every gesture he made, was recorded by supersensitive electronic devices that scanned the corridor more intensively than a hundred human sentries could have done. The ability to travel to other dimensions was the most closely guarded secret in England, one that millions of pounds and a few lives had been spent to protect. Not even England's friends could be trusted with the secret of what Lord Leighton had done, and as for her enemies—

A thought struck Blade. "Is Lord Leighton planning any special effects for me this time?"

J shook his head. His voice held a mixture of relief and annoyance as he said, "There's really nothing ready to test that hasn't already failed. Lord Leighton doesn't dare make your trips too much more unpredictable than they already are!"

"No," said Blade. "For better or worse, I'm his indispensable man."

That was really doing the brilliant little scientist something of an injustice. Leighton normally had more regard for his computers than for any ten thousand human beings. But he did have some regard for Richard Blade, and it wasn't entirely the result of Blade's being indispensable to Project Dimension X. The scientist would rather have his budget canceled than admit it, but where Blade was concerned he almost had a heart.

"No, this time it's just a simple trip," J continued. "Go out, and do your best to come back."

That was just as well, all things considered. Sooner or later they would have to develop the ability to send Blade off to a specific dimension at will. And they would also have to stop landing Blade in Dimension X as naked as a newborn babe. And finally, they would have to learn to bring back from Dimension X more than what happened to be on or around Blade at the moment the computer gripped him for the return trip.

All of these things would be necessary if the project were ever to repay the millions of pounds it had swallowed up since its beginning. But in spite of all the time and money spent trying to do them, nothing much had happened. Even the trials had mostly just made Blade's trips more dangerous—and even Lord Leighton agreed that a trip into Dimension X was hair-raising enough at the best of times.

Besides, if Blade were killed, everything would come to a screeching halt. All the efforts to find even one other person who could travel into Dimension X and return alive and sane had also fallen flat.

So Blade was for now indeed the indispensable man for a project vital to England's future. It was not a status he enjoyed, although by temperament he was a natural adventurer.

As they approached the door into the computer rooms, Lord Leighton came out to meet them. He scuttled up to them on his polio-twisted legs, holding out a hand whose long, thin fingers were still surprisingly strong and skilled.

"Good morning, Richard. J's told you we're not putting any icing on your cake this time."

"Yes, sir. He did." After a pause, Blade said, "I sometimes wonder if we're not going to solve some of our problems by accident. We'll have given up any hope of finding a solution, and then suddenly one will leap out at us. Then all the sub-projects—"

Leighton shot Blade a venomous look, as if the younger man had just confessed to poisoning babies for a living. Blade managed to keep a grin off his face. Leighton believed almost religiously that the systematic application of the scientific method could solve any problem. Blade and J, on the other hand, had been professionals in the intelligence business. That was a business that ran as much by accident and educated guesswork as by any sort of system.

Now they were passing through a succession of rooms filled with supporting equipment, terminals, and white-coated technicians bending over them. There were three or four of those rooms—Blade had never bothered to count them exactly. Then finally they were in the heart of the whole complex, the main computer room.

The monstrous main computer towered toward the bare rock ceiling. The gray, crackled finish of the ranked consoles gave off no reflections, even from the harsh lighting. Blade walked over to the metal chair that stood in its glass booth in the middle of the chamber and looked down at it.

Then quickly he stepped into the small changing room in one corner of the chamber and stripped himself to the skin. Just as quickly, but much more carefully, he smeared himself all over with foul-smelling, black, greasy cream. Then he pulled on a loincloth and stepped back out into the chamber.

The rubber seat and back of the chair were as chilly as ever against his bare skin. Lord Leighton bustled about, busily attaching the mass of cobra-headed electrodes whose multicolored wires linked Blade to the computer. There seemed to be more of them than usual. Or was it just his impatience to be off that was making the wiring-up process seem longer?

Eventually there were no more. J raised his hand in a final salute to Blade, then withdrew to the small folding chair that had been installed on the wall for him. Lord Leighton stepped up to the main control panel, lifting his hand over the red master switch.

Blade suddenly felt an impish and almost uncontrollable desire to say something memorably scandalous, something that would have turned Lord Leighton's remaining hair white if it hadn't been white already. Then he fought down the desire. They didn't know much about Dimension X. But they had begun to suspect that what Blade was thinking about at the moment of transition might be connected with where he wound up. So it might not be wise to go sailing off into Dimension X with a bawdy joke on his mind.

Then Lord Leighton drew the master switch downward in its slot. The chamber vanished.

For a moment the after-image lingered in Blade's vision. It lingered so vividly that for another moment he doubted whether he had even started the transition. Something had gone wrong; he was still in the chamber below the Tower, and Lord Leighton—

Then he realized that he was standing alone and naked in the middle of an immense, dark red plain. As far as his eyes could reach it was the color of old blood and as featureless as a tabletop. Above it arched a totally black sky, without a single star. There was no wind, no feeling of either heat or cold, and a silence that could not have been more complete if Blade had been marooned in outer space.

The silent red plain and the silent black sky were beginning to become oppressive when Blade noticed something high in the sky, directly above his head. A pulsating spot of raw, rich gold appeared in the sky. Then the spot began to rotate. It whirled faster and faster, throwing out long streamers down toward the horizon.

The golden streamers reached the horizon. As they did so, the plain under Blade's feet began to rotate in turn, slowly at first, then faster and faster, until it was matching the speed of the golden spot high above.

The golden streamers began to waver and dance wildly, shimmering and hurling sparks and bits of fire down out of the sky like meteors. The plain under Blade's feet whirled faster and faster. Now it began to quiver like a driven piece of machinery and give out a high-pitched hum.

Still faster. Blade began to feel a weight pressing on his chest, making it hard to breathe. He tried to raise one hand to shade his eyes against the fire from the golden streamers. His arm seemed to weigh a ton.

He looked down and saw that his feet were beginning to flow, melting into the plain like hot wax under the weight pressing down on him. His feet went, then his ankles, then he was standing on fast-dissolving knees. He melted up as far as the waist, stayed there for a moment, then continued to vanish. In seconds he could no longer see how far his body had spread, for the horizon was getting closer and closer as he shrank down and melted into the plain. In a few more seconds all that was left was his head, his chin resting on the plain itself. Somehow he managed to raise his eyes for a final look at the nightmarish dance of the golden streamers against the black sky.

Then his head dissolved, and there was only blackness.

3

Blade's first sensation was the usual pounding headache that followed a transition into Dimension X. It proved that he was alive, and it always went away after a few minutes. Meanwhile the best plan was to lie quietly. Blade cautiously opened his eyes and looked around him.

A chilly wind was blowing over him and whistling in the tops of nearby trees, and mist swirled above him. Under his naked body he could feel a thick layer of dead needles and leaves on rocky soil. He was lying with his feet higher than his aching head, which lay between the half-exposed roots of a tree that soared up into the gray mist. A branch heavy with long green needles hung down almost to Blade's nose, arching and curving as the brisk wind tossed it. There was no sight or sound or smell of anything dangerous, human or animal. Blade decided to go on lying still until his head cleared.

The fresh air helped, and soon Blade could stand up. He stepped around the tree to get its thick trunk between himself and the wind and took a more thorough look around.

The dense forest and the swirling gray mist cut off his vision close at hand—sometimes to only a few yards. But he could see enough to gather that he was in rugged, heavily forested country. It looked like uninhabited, almost virgin wilderness.

It was pointless to try to tell the time of day as long as the mist cut off the view. But if it was this raw and cold by day, Blade had no intention of staying out here to face the night in the forest, naked and alone. He was tough enough to do it if he had to, but exhaustion from exposure could leave him less able to fight or run. Much better to find whoever lived in this dimension, get fed, get warm, and start learning his way around. *If* anybody lived in this dimension. So far he had never landed in a totally uninhabited dimension, but there was always a first time for—

This dimension would not be it. Before Blade could complete the thought, an unmistakably artificial sound came floating down to his ears. Somewhere, apparently close upwind, someone was beating a large gong. Blade listened more carefully. A *very* large gong. Its notes had a deep, booming quality, and went on and on and on, fading away only gradually. Each note had barely time to die away before another followed on its heels.

The gong seemed to be somewhere farther up the hill. Blade peered as intently as he could at the forest above, but the trees grew so thickly that it was like trying to peer through a brick wall. Blade gave up the effort and struck off uphill, letting the sound of the gong guide him over the rough ground.

The gong fell silent before Blade had covered more than two hundred yards. But barely fifty yards farther on, he saw a double line of white stones gleaming ahead in the twilight. He froze until he was reasonably sure there was no one within sight or earshot. Then he slipped forward to stand by the nearer line of stones.

As he had suspected, the stones marked out a path of bare earth, beaten almost rock-hard by the passage of many feet over many years. The path ran up and down the hill, rapidly losing itself in the mist and shadows under the trees in either direction. Blade looked toward the top of the hill and thought he could see a dark mass looming through the trees, a dark mass too regular in shape to be a natural feature.

So he headed uphill, following the line of the path but far enough from it so that the white stones were barely visible. He didn't want to unexpectedly meet whoever used the path.

The slope soon became noticeably steeper and the undergrowth not only more tangled, but thorny. By the time Blade reached the top, he was sweating heavily in spite of the chill. Blood from dozens of places where the thorns had jabbed him ran down his legs, arms, and chest. He stripped a handful of wet leaves off a nearby bush and used them to wipe off his body while he looked at the building on top of the hill.

It rose a good sixty feet above the wall that surrounded it on three sides and had a distinctly Oriental flavor. It looked like a mass of heavily tiled overhanging roofs, heavy beams carved in elaborate floral designs, gilded dragons' heads, and small windows with even more elaborately carved shutters. The protecting wall was eight feet high, overgrown with thorny vines and creepers, and surmounted with a double row of foot-long iron spikes. On one side of the building a rather rickety-looking mass of scaffolding rose halfway to the top floor, but there was nobody on it.

In fact, there was nobody in sight around the entire building. The fourth side of the enclosure was wide open except for a solid wooden hut about twenty feet square blocking off part of it. Blade could see almost the entire space within the walls. Most of it was laid out with delicately pruned shrubs between white gravel paths and small pools, but there was nobody in it. The building—a temple, probably—seemed deserted.

That was obviously impossible. Behind the hut stood a bronze gong at least nine feet in diameter, hanging on a heavy frame of blackish brown wood. Somebody had been beating that gong not more than twenty minutes ago. Where had they gone? Perhaps there was only a caretaker in the hut, who beat the gong at regular intervals for some religious reason and had now gone back into the hut to get out of the weather.

That seemed likely enough. Blade decided to explore further. He was going to need to get out of the weather himself, sooner or later. So he headed straight in, walking carefully so that his bare feet made no sound on the gravel.

In the rear of the temple, out of sight of the hut, Blade stopped and looked again. A small, polished door with a gilded, many-rayed bronze sun on it let him into the temple itself. Inside was darkness that smelled of varnish, old wood, dust, and incense. A narrow flight of stairs rose upward and vanished.

The second floor was a single, large, bare chamber, its walls and floor both whitewashed. In one corner was a pile of what seemed to be temple gear—brass and porcelain urns, censers on gilded chains, screens, mats, small lacquered boxes, and assorted bamboolike poles of various lengths. Blade picked up an eight-foot pole and tested it for balance and ease of handling. It wasn't much of a weapon, even for a quarter-staff expert like Blade. But it was a damned sight better than bare hands!

Blade was turning toward the stairs to the third floor when he heard the gong sounding again from below. It sounded eight times, in two groups of four beats. As the echoes of the last beat faded away into the forest, Blade heard quick, light footsteps descending the stairs from above. He froze, realized there was no place to hide in the room, and dashed for the stairs leading down.

Before he could get out of sight, a woman appeared at the foot of the stairs from the third floor and froze to stare in amazement at Blade. She wore a blue and white patterned kimonolike robe with a golden sash and a large, gold-lacquered mask shoved up onto the top of her head. In one hand she carried a blue porcelain urn and in the other a small, gilded bronze censer on a chain.

Before Blade could move or speak, the woman leaped violently to one side. The leap carried her halfway to the pile of temple gear. As she landed she let out a raw, wordless screech that sounded more like a wildcat than anything human. Then she ran to the open window on the side of the building toward the hut and screamed:

"Blasphemy! Blasphemy! A madman in the Temple of Kunkoi! A naked madman! Avenge the honor of the goddess!"

Blade raised the bamboo pole. The woman spun around and hurled the urn straight at Blade's head. He ducked, just in time for the urn to sail past his ear and smash into the wall behind him. From the crash it made, he knew that it would have smashed his skull if it had connected. Then the priestess was advancing on him, swinging the censer around and around her head on its chain. Not wildly, like a panic-stricken woman, but like someone who knew very well what she was doing and had trained for years with the weapon she was using.

Blade held his ground. If he could disarm the woman without hurting her, perhaps he could— The woman suddenly let out another foot of chain, and the censer whirled close enough to Blade to make him jump back.

He raised his pole, ready to thrust it into the circle and entangle the whirling chain. But as fast as Blade moved, the woman moved just as fast. She swung the censer low, snagging the lower end of Blade's pole. Then she threw herself backward in a complete somersault, putting all of her weight and all her strength behind the pull on the chain. The pole leaped out of Blade's hands, smashing him across the left cheek as it did so, and flew like a spear across the room. Before he could recover, the woman was back on her feet. She snatched up another pole from the pile with one hand and drew a short, curved dagger from her sash with the other.

Then from outside came the booming of the gong. It was sounding in a rapid beat. Along with the gong came the rattle of doors and weapons, the scrape of running feet on gravel, and shouted orders. The temple's guards were turning out in answer to the priestess' call. It went against Blade's instincts to run like a rabbit, but he didn't see what else to do. He couldn't face the guards barehanded until he got some maneuvering room. That meant getting out of the temple, for a starter.

Blade plunged down the stairs three at a time. The priestess followed close on his heels, waving her dagger and shouting at the top of her lungs, "Blasphemer! Slay, slay, slay for the honor of Kunkoi!"

As Blade reached the foot of the stairs the temple door flew open and a spear whistled past his nose and chunked into the wall behind him. By pure reflex he whirled, jerked the spear loose, and jabbed it butt-first at the priestess as she came within range. She jumped aside, Blade whirled the spear over and around, then slammed the shaft across the back of her knees. She went down the last four steps with a screech and a clatter of wooden clogs, sprawling face-down on the floor. Her dagger flew out of her hand and went spinning away.

Blade bent to pick it up. As he did so, the first guard came charging through the open door. In the close quarters and the dim light the man looked at least seven feet tall and six feet wide; he must have been a good deal bigger than Blade. He gave a yell of fury as he saw the priestess sprawled on the floor and charged straight at Blade. As he came he snatched a six-foot curved sword from a scabbard across his back and sent it whistling down toward Blade.

Blade swung his spear around in front of him and held it out to block the stroke. If the guard had been able to let loose a full swing, the sword would have split Blade down the middle as neatly as a barbecued chicken. But the low ceiling saved him. The sword whistled down in front of him, effortlessly chopping his spear in two.

Now Blade had the advantage for a moment, the advantage any good fighting man has at close quarters against an opponent with a two-handed weapon. He used that advantage, feinting at the guard's groin with the severed point of his spear. The guard took his eyes off Blade's other hand for a second, long enough for Blade to ram the butt of the spear straight up under his chin. The guard reeled and toppled with a crash that seemed to shake the whole temple.

Behind him Blade heard the priestess getting to her feet, still screeching, "Slay the blasphemer! Avenge the honor of the Sun Goddess!" Having no desire to be slain to avenge the honor of the Sun Goddess, or for any other reason, Blade dashed out of the temple like a sprinter trying to set a world's record.

He was rounding the corner of the temple on the side where the scaffolding stood when he met six guards coming the other way. They all carried spears and the long curved swords, and wore cotton coats and kilts sewn with small iron discs and lacquered-metal hats and greaves. None of them was much smaller than the one Blade had disabled inside the temple, and all of them looked just as unfriendly.

Blade had a brief feeling that this was the end of the road for him. But it wasn't in him to die tamely. He grabbed at one of the poles in the scaffolding, jerking it loose and raising it high. If he could keep the guards at bay long enough to explain himself—

Before he could complete the thought, a sharp crack sounded from high overhead. One of the guards jerked his head upward, then gave a yell of fear and turned to run. The other guards froze in their tracks. Blade risked a quick look of his own—just as the whole scaffolding shivered, shook, and then began to collapse.

Poles and cross-braces snapped and cracked, tiles, planks, pots of paint, and varnish showered down like hailstones, and the guards scattered in all directions. Blade jumped back too, but not quite fast enough. A pot of paint came plummeting down and scored a direct hit on his left shoulder. It disintegrated as it struck, barely bruising the skin but drenching Blade's chest and left arm with oily brown paint.

As the wreckage settled Blade looked toward the entrance. The guards were forming a line across it, so there would be no getting out that way. It would have to be over the walls and then outrun the guards. The second part wouldn't be hard—they didn't look built for speed. But the first part—well, there was the pole in his hands. Blade hefted it and flexed it. It would have to do.

He moved back as far as possible to give himself a longer run. He could only hope that the guards wouldn't realize what he was doing until it was too late. He threw a quick look back over his shoulder.

Good. They apparently thought they had him trapped.

Now—raise the pole, take a deep breath—several deep breaths—and RUN!

Blade charged toward the wall even faster than he had gone out of the temple. His long legs ate up the ground. As he judged the right second, the pole swung down in a long arc, driving down into the ground as Blade drove upward with all the strength in his body. Blade felt himself soaring upward, rising up to the level of the spikes on top of the wall, rising over them—

Crack! The pole slammed into the wall and snapped like a twig, twisting Blade in midair. He flung himself over into a complete somersault, desperately trying to avoid landing headfirst. By a minor miracle he managed to land rolling, on his shoulders and back. He kept rolling, doing another complete somersault and leaping to his feet at the end. Five careful deep breaths, and he was off down the hill, ignoring all the bruises and scrapes and twinges in his protesting muscles. He did not run blindly, like a panic-stricken animal. He ran like a distance runner, pacing himself for the best combination of speed and endurance.

He hoped his guess was right about those temple guards not being built or trained for running.

4

Blade never found out whether the guards came after him or not. They would have had a job catching up with him if they had. He kept on at a steady lope for nearly half an hour, heading downhill as much as possible. When his breath began to come short, he slowed down to an equally steady jog. He kept that up for another full hour. By that time he estimated he was at least six miles from the temple and decided it was safe enough to stop and rest. He badly needed to catch his breath and reorient himself. He didn't want to wind up marching steadily away from civilization, on top of everything else that had gone wrong since he had arrived in this dimension. So far about the only things he had done right were not getting himself killed and not killing anybody else. For all he knew, the affair at the temple might even now have the guards scattering all over the countryside, with a description of him and a "kill this man on sight" order.

So he rested just long enough to catch his breath and get some of the aches out of his legs. Then he was on his feet again and on his way downhill. Sooner or later going downhill should bring him to civilization. He had never heard of a people who built *all* their homes on the tops of the hills and none in the valleys.

He had been walking for about another hour when

it started to rain, a miserable, chill drizzle that soon strengthened into an even more miserable and chillier downpour. The rain made some of the caked and smeared brown paint run, so that before long he looked like the victim of some particularly repulsive skin disease. Blade was too disgusted and almost too tired to even swear at this.

It was beginning to get dark when Blade finally came out on the bank of a small, swift stream tumbling downhill through a series of pools and rapids. Unmistakable paths ran along both banks of the stream. Blade nearly let out a cheer, and then swallowed it as the sound of human voices reached him over the patter of the rain and the gurgle of water boiling over the stones.

It was women singing—or rather, chanting rhythmically. Their voices were punctuated by wet, slapping noises. Blade slipped silently through fifty feet of trees and dripping bushes, then crouched and watched even more silently.

Two half-nude young women—hardly more than girls, judging from their slight figures—squatted on the edge of the stream, washing clothes and singing to themselves as they worked. They pounded each garment on a convenient rock to get the dirt out and then spread it out on one of the bushes behind them. Blade saw loincloths, long socks, sashes and scarves, and more of the kimonolike robes in half a dozen different styles and colors. If he could just sneak in and make a quick grab, his clothing problem at least would be solved.

Blade had once made it safely through a Communist minefield with a sixty-pound pack on his back, so there wasn't much he had to learn about moving silently and carefully. Inch by inch he crept closer, belly flat to the ground most of the time, raising his head to take an occasional bearing. It took him five minutes to cover five yards. By the time he did, all his bruises and strained muscles were protesting angrily. His spine felt as though it were going to snap with a crack loud enough to alert the women.

Two yards more. Then he had to freeze for what seemed like an hour, as one of the women sat down to rest with her eyes on the spread-out clothes. Blade lay motionless, gritting his teeth to stifle a grunt of impatience, wondering if the woman would ever get up off her arse!

It seemed like an hour, but it couldn't have been more than five minutes before the woman stood up and began unwrapping the cloth around her waist. It fell to the ground, and she stepped naked down into the pool. As the other woman turned to do the same Blade snaked forward the last few feet, and his long arms reached out. In seconds he gathered in a long blue robe, a red sash, and a loincloth. In a few more seconds he was back under the bushes, crawling away as fast as he could. The two girls were still splashing about cheerfully in the pool, completely unconcerned with what might be going on around them.

A quarter of a mile later, Blade stopped to put on the clothes and get his bearings again. The loincloth was plain linen, but the sash seemed to be heavy red silk, with stylized waves embroidered on it in white thread. The blue robe was also linen, light but fine and tough, with elaborate patterns of black and white checks embroidered around the neck, bottom, and cuffs. On the right sleeve about halfway to the elbow was a stylized golden sunburst with sixteen rays picked out in red.

For all its elegance, the garment had obviously been made for someone rather shorter and slimmer than Blade. From the cut it was obviously intended to be fought in, but it made Blade feel more like a sausage stuffed into its skin. Oh, well, he could always strip it off if he had to fight or run again.

He guessed that there must be a house nearby if the girls had felt safe washing and bathing alone by the stream, as they obviously had. It would probably be downstream, too. The water in the stream would be cleaner above the house.

Blade had guessed right. A few minutes walking, and he saw a large house and the glow of lanterns through the forest and the rain. The house was on the far side of the stream, but a gracefully arched wooden bridge provided an easy crossing.

The house itself was a sprawling, one-story affair, with several wings apparently running off at odd angles to each other and a massive tile roof that seemed too heavy for the building under it. Blade saw no one moving outside, but he could see the glow of lights through the delicate lattice-work shutters over the windows. From the rear rose a column of smoke, coiling upward slowly until it disintegrated under the rain.

Blade darted across the bridge and began working his way around the house toward the rear. That smoke might mean the kitchen, and that was the place he intended to start. The chill weather and his exertions during the day had made Blade hungry enough to eat a colt, if not a full-grown horse.

As he reached the rear of the house, the appetizing sound and even more appetizing smell of frying food drifted out to greet him. He stood up and tied the sash more neatly around his waist. He couldn't be sure exactly what class or rank his robe indicated, but he suspected it was something well up the social scale—possibly even the local warrior caste. Blade's experience with warrior castes in several different dimensions had taught him that they always carried themselves with a swagger. So he drew himself up to his full six feet one as he approached the kitchen door and knocked as sharply as if he were a policeman. It never hurt to look and sound as though you had every right to be where you were and to be doing what you were doing.

The door opened after Blade's third knock. An old woman peered out, her wrinkled but sharp brown features screwed up into an angry frown. Then she took in Blade's commanding height, his air of calm arrogance, and his robe. Her expression changed in a split second to one of abashed servility. She dropped to her knees, beat her head three times on the ground with her hands over her eyes, and then straightened up.

"What is your wish, Honorable *dabuno*?"

"My wish is food." Blade kept his voice cold and haughty.

"Food, yes. Do you wish anything else?"

"We will speak of that after the food." And after he had taken a look around.

"It shall be so." The woman's voice had an almost ritual quality as she spoke. Then she stood up, bowed low, and led Blade inside.

The kitchen was lit by several lanterns and the glowing bed of charcoal under the heavy iron grate on the stone hearth. On that grate stood several large iron pots and an iron pan at least a yard in diameter. What looked like enough meat and vegetables to feed a battalion sizzled cheerfully in the pan, and clouds of sweet-smelling steam rose from the pots. Blade kept his face straight, but he could not keep his stomach from giving off a rumble like a tank engine.

There was a mat in one corner of the kitchen. Blade sat down cross-legged on it. Strains, sprains, and bruises protested as he did so. He realized that he would have to get thoroughly thawed out, and fast. Otherwise he would be stiff enough tomorrow to be slowed down in a fight. That could be fatal.

The curtain across the door leading into the main area of the house was pushed open, and a young woman came in with a stack of dirty dishes. Blade's eyes flickered across her, recognizing her as one of the women by the stream, scanning her for any sign that she suspected anything. But she bowed as the old woman had done when she saw the blue robe, then she murmured, "The house of the Honorable Captain Jawai is honored by your presence, *dabuno*."

Blade merely nodded graciously. Then the old woman came over with a lacquered tray holding a bowl of soup, a bowl of meat and vegetables, and a large plate of coarse, whitish porridge. The only eating utensils visible were six-sided lacquered sticks, enough like chopsticks so that Blade could use them easily. He dug into the food with no effort to conceal his hunger. Perhaps the *dabuni* were supposed to be ascetics who picked at their food, but at the moment he didn't care. He could argue that or any other point much better with a full meal in his stomach.

Neither of the women made any comment on the rate at which Blade emptied his tray, nor raised an eyebrow when he asked for more. The young woman only asked, "Do you also wish *saya*?"

Whatever that was, it sounded alcoholic. Blade shook his head. After a long and exceptionally exhausting day that might still end violently, he wanted to stay absolutely sober.

"Ah, I see you have taken the *dem* vow as well as becoming a Lonely Brother," said the older woman. "Then you will not wish to meet the Honorable Captain Jawai?"

Blade had been wondering how to get out of going through any social formalities with the master of the house. But now the woman had just presented him with what seemed like a ready-made excuse.

"Yes, I have taken the *dem* vow." The paint on his skin was beginning to itch. He pulled the robe half off his left shoulder and rubbed vigorously. He would have to ask for some turpentine or something to get this muck off before long.

The girl's eyes widened at the width and muscles of Blade's chest. The old woman noticed where the girl was looking and slapped her lightly on the shoulder. "Don't make eyes at a Lonely Brother who has taken the *dem* vow, Kika. He's not for you." Blade decided he should nod again at those words. "Now go and tell the Honorable Captain about our guest."

Kika vanished through the curtain, still looking back at Blade. Blade looked at his empty tray, considered whether he should eat any more, and decided against it. The food and the warmth would be making him feel sleepy before long.

Blade's tray had barely touched the mats on the floor when a sharp, shrill scream sounded from farther inside the house. Then the girl's voice—"No, Honorable Master, please. I did not know!"—the sound of two hard blows, another scream, and the thud of a falling body.

Blade was on his feet before the first scream died away, his eyes flickering around the room for a safe spot and a weapon of some sort. One leap carried him into the opposite corner, where he had both flanks protected by heavily timbered walls. As he moved he snatched up the poker leaning against the hearth. Then before the old woman could move or even open her mouth for a scream of her own, he scooped up her carving knife with the other hand.

He had barely regained his safe corner when more noises came from inside the house. First the clatter of falling trays and bowls, then the hissing sound of a sword being drawn, finally the thud of fast-moving feet heading toward the kitchen. Blade crouched low, raised the poker to guard, and held the carving knife ready to thrust.

A moment later the curtain flew open, and another man in a blue robe burst into the kitchen. Both hands held a curved, yard-long sword above his head. The light shimmered on the flawlessly polished steel, and another kind of light gleamed in his eyes. It was the light of an almost maniacal determination to kill or die.

Blade had braced himself physically for an attack. Now he quickly braced himself mentally for a fight to the death.

5

The sword whistled down. Blade angled the poker downward to make the sword strike it a glancing blow. He suspected that an overhead slash from that sword would hack through even the tough iron of the poker.

The sword came down, struck with a terrific clang, and glanced off. But the other man swung it up into position again almost faster than Blade's eye could follow. Blade shifted his grip on the poker, now holding it upright. His opponent was watching him more closely now. The man's eyes were still filled with rage and also now with curiosity. That made him more dangerous. He might not swing in wild fury again, but use his skill instead. The sword seemed to hover, the light glinting from it.

Blade never found out what the man would have done next. The curtain burst open again and another man in a shorter and plainer blue robe dashed into the kitchen. He took up a position by the door, bowed quickly to the first man, and drew his own sword. The first man nodded. Blade saw his hands tighten on his sword.

Then the curtain flew open a third time. Blade had a moment's glimpse of a slim figure, clad only in wide black trousers and carrying his drawn sword in front of him. Then the second swordsman whirled to confront the new arrival. The new arrival's sword seemed to leap toward the ceiling like a living thing, the blade reaching up and slicing the air as though trying to bring down a bird on the wing. The other's sword started to follow it. Then the first sword came down as fast as it had gone up, slashing from the side. There was a sound like a butcher chopping meat and a gasping grunt from the second swordsman. He dropped his sword, staggered, twisting completely around, and toppled to the floor. Blood sprayed out through the slash that had cut him open from armpit to breastbone, and some of it sprayed onto the hearth. The pungent smell of burning human blood rose into the room.

The old woman gasped and tottered. Blade reached out and clamped one hand on the neck of her robe to keep her from toppling into the fire. His opponent made no effort to take advantage of his moment's distraction. Instead he turned to look at the newcomer. After a moment Blade did the same.

The newcomer was a young man—his bare chest and arms were layered with sinewy muscles, but the face above it was almost boyish. Blade wondered if he was much more than twenty or so. He bent to wipe his sword on the robe of his victim, then sheathed it and crossed his arms on his chest.

"Honorable Captain Jawai, what is your purpose in this fight?" His voice was as quiet as that of a man ordering a drink in a conservative London club, and it carried the same tone—he was unquestionably expecting a proper answer. It subdued Jawai, who sheathed his own sword and bowed low. Blade realized that the newcomer might not be his friend, but he did not seem a friend of Jawai either.

"This man," said Jawai, jerking his head at Blade. "This—dirty lout—blasphemed the Igumasi Temple of Kunkoi, assaulting both the priestess and the guards. He then fled, and apparently stole the robe of a *da-*

buno from one of my servants while she was washing it in the stream earlier this evening."

The young swordsman nodded. "I recognize the robe he is wearing."

"Word came from the temple by messenger to look for a very tall and strong man, paleskinned but probably with paint smeared on his chest. The servant-girl Kika told me that a Lonely Brother just like that was in the kitchen, saying that he was under the *dem* vow. I forced her to confess the loss of your robe and punished her for it."

"I heard," said the young man.

"Then I entered the kitchen, to kill the blasphemer and avenge the honor of Kunkoi. What happened after that you know well." Jawai could not keep the anger entirely out of his voice as he finished.

The young man nodded slowly. "Was the temple damaged in any way, or any blood shed in the precincts?"

"A scaffolding fell down, and the captain of the guards was knocked unconscious. But—"

"So the temple is intact, and blood is unshed?"

Jawai nodded reluctantly. "That is as I was told."

"Then the blasphemy is one that can be compounded with gold, if the priestesses of Kunkoi give their consent."

"But he is still guilty of falsely wearing the robe of a *dabuno*," exploded Jawai, clapping his hand to his sword hilt. "No gold may sweep aside that crime."

"If he has committed it, no," said the young man slowly. He fixed his eyes on Blade. Blade saw in those eyes an assurance and an authority surprising in a man so young. "I am Yezjaro, instructor to the Warlord Tsekuin. Tell me in your own words what happened at the temple of Kunkoi."

Blade ran through the story as quickly as possible, trying to keep an eye on both Jawai and Yezjaro at the same time as he talked. When he had finished, Yezjaro looked at him closely.

"You entered the temple precincts by accident?"

"Entirely by accident. I thought it was deserted or at least not being used at the time."

"And you neither slew nor maimed any of the temple's people?"

"I did my best not to," said Blade. "If they had stopped to listen to me, I would have told them just what I've told you and then departed. The priestess fell down some steps and I had to knock the guard captain down to save my own life. Other than that I don't see how anybody could have been hurt."

"You seem to have skill and self-control, as well as courage," said Yezjaro. Blade thought it appropriate to bow in response to this praise. Yezjaro smiled. "But what of your wearing the robe of a *dabuno*? That is another and graver crime, as Captain Jawai has said."

Blade thought quickly. "I am sorry that it was your robe. But it was a garment appropriate to my rank in my own land." He ran quickly through a story of his origins, his travels, and his arrival in this land.

"So in a sense I am indeed of the rank of *dabuno*, traveling as a Lonely Brother, and I have taken the *dem* vow. But this is by the laws and customs of my own land. I know yours are different, and I submit to being judged by them."

There was a long silence. It seemed even longer to Blade. Finally Yezjaro clasped both hands behind his back and looked down at the floor for a moment. Then he looked at Blade again.

"It is not beyond belief that you are a warrior, considering what you seem to have done. Were you of the land of Gaikon, I think I would accept your story. I would then pay for having a new robe of *dabuno* rank made for you, as mine fits you like a man's sash on an ox!" He laughed briefly at his own joke, then sobered. "If you lied, you would be discovered sooner or later and punished terribly. If not by men here in Gaikon, then by the Goddess Kunkoi after your death.

"But you are from a distant land, known only to Kunkoi, with customs and laws of which we know only what you chose to tell us. Who knows if you fear Kunkoi's judgment? So I cannot accept your word."

His eyes dropped to the poker and knife Blade was still holding. "Would it be acceptable to you to fight against Captain Jawai with a weapon of your choice? He is an excellent swordsman, of the fourth *Kju*. If you can defeat him or even last more than a few minutes against him, it will satisfy me that you indeed deserve to be accepted as a *dabuno* in Gaikon. Then–"

"It won't satisfy me!" snapped Jawai. "What if he asks for some weapon we can't give him? Or fights with a bow? What if–?"

"I did not finish, Captain," said Yezjaro. His voice would have frozen an entire side of beef in a split second. "The fight will take place as I say. Unless you wish to try defeating me first?" One long-fingered hand dropped to the hilt of his own sword.

Jawai gulped, apparently realizing his danger for the first time. "No, Honorable Instructor, I do not wish to disobey your wishes in this matter." Then rage got the better of his self-control. "But you've always been after me, one way or another. You're using this–"

Yezjaro sighed. "Captain, I advise you not to open your mouth again except to shout a challenge. Otherwise I shall have to tell Lord Tsekuin that you dishonor the name of his clan. Then you will pass from among us without ever having the chance to prove that you speak the truth about this man."

Apparently the prospect of dying a condemned liar

and loudmouth was enough to subdue even Jawai's flapping tongue. He swallowed and bowed almost humbly.

"Good," said Yezjaro. "Now, stranger, you may choose any weapon that is to be found readily in Gaikon. What is your choice?"

Blade thought furiously and fast. He wished he could ask a few questions about the weaponry and weapons etiquette of a *dabuno* of Gaikon. But he couldn't be sure if he could trust Yezjaro that far. The clan's instructor seemed to be a formidable and knowledgeable young fighter. But he was also filled with a youthful arrogance and pride that might make him rather unbending. In general, he was not the man Blade would have chosen for his first ally in Gaikon if he had had a choice. But he didn't, so that was that.

"I have seen spears much used," said Blade. "I will fight with one of those." He knew just about everything that could be done with any sort of spear. And he knew just enough about the Japanese sword, the *katana*—which the swords of Gaikon resembled—to know that it would take him a year of practice before he could fight well with one of them.

"Very good," said Yezjaro. "The Honorable Captain Jawai will fight with his sword. Now I suggest we summon servants with torches to light the battle and some of the *dabuni* to act as witnesses. Then we shall go outside."

"Why?" asked Jawai.

Yezjaro laughed. "Consider how many holes a war spear might make in your roof, Captain. Do you want the rain dripping in on your mats and furniture like a dog's piss?" He laughed again, and was still laughing as he led the other two men out of the kitchen.

6

As young as Yezjaro was, he was obviously accustomed to giving orders and getting obedience even from the households of other *dabuni* in Lord Tsekuin's service. Servants ran about with his various messages while he himself led Blade to Jawai's weapons room. The low-ceilinged room was lined with rack after rack of swords, spears, shields of lacquered wood and metal, complicated suits of armor like the shell of a lobster in black, red, and blue lacquered metal, and a miscellany of other war gear.

Yezjaro went over to a rack, took one of the spears, and held it out to Blade. "For a man of your height, this would seem to be the best."

Blade hefted the spear. It balanced well, and although both shaft and head were fine steel, it was so light he could whirl it with one hand until it was a blur. It had a leaf-shaped head about a foot long, and about six inches behind the head two prongs jutted out and forward. Blade stepped out into the middle of the room and tested the spear in every possible position. By the time he felt he knew it, he had also limbered up all his sore muscles without fatiguing himself.

Yezjaro watched with a sardonically amused smile flickering on his lips. When Blade had finished he clapped him on the shoulder and said, "I think Captain Jawai faces more of a fight than he is ready to believe. It will be interesting to watch him when he discovers this."

Blade suspected Yezjaro was looking forward to being greatly entertained by the coming fight, regardless of who won. He rather wished he could manage the same detached view of the affair.

The place chosen for the fight was a clearing among some huts in the forest several hundred yards uphill from the main house. When Blade and Yezjaro arrived, a dozen servants were already at work. Some crawled on hands and knees across a square marked out in the grass by four white stones, picking up rocks and fallen branches. The rest stood around the square, holding flickering yellow torches that threw out only a little light and a great deal of smoke and smell.

The rain had faded away to a fine misting, but it was almost completely dark and the wind had risen. It moaned continuously to itself in the treetops high above, occasionally rising to an angry howl. The sounds of the wind, the darkness, and the flickering torchlight that made the servants look deformed and misshapen lent an eerie and sinister quality to the place. It seemed far too appropriate for death.

Blade had given back Yezjaro's robe and was wearing a pair of broad white trousers with green embroidery across the waistband. Otherwise he wore nothing except a red silk band around his head.

The servants finished their work and Yezjaro nodded to Blade. Blade stepped out into the middle of the square and began testing the footing. He had barely finished when the beating of a small gong and the tinkling of bells announced the arrival of several of the house *dabuni.* Behind them marched—or rather strutted—the Honorable Captain Jawai. He wore black trousers and a white headband and carried two swords in the sash around his lean waist. Blade wished he knew whether the shorter of the two swords was ceremonial or not. He decided to assume that it wasn't. That was always the safest assumption about any weapon that an enemy carried into battle against you.

The house *dabuni* formed a line between the square and the huts and drew their swords. Jawai stepped through the line. His sword flew free, the torchlight making flowing patterns of light on the steel. He raised it high over his head, keeping the point down. Blade heard Yezjaro's indrawn breath behind him and saw the other *dabuni* grin. Apparently Jawai had just insulted him. Blade grinned, shifted his spear to one hand, and made the almost universal gesture of biting his thumb at Jawai. The captain's face clouded and his sword flicked back into its scabbard as he spat on the ground. Then he raised his hand and called out to Blade.

"Pray to whatever false gods you imagine will listen, imposter. I will give you as much time as you need to bore them with your whines and howls for the mercy you shall not have."

Blade bared his teeth in a grin, tossed his spear up into the air, and caught it between the thumb and forefinger of his left hand, "I trust in Blessed Kunkoi, who rules justly in this land of Gaikon. And I trust in these,"—he made the heavy muscles of his arms and chest ripple. "Let us do what we came here for, and let it be judged afterwards which of us had the favor of Kunkoi or the greater need for prayers."

"So be it," said Yezjaro. He stepped out from behind Blade and crossed the square to stand in front of the line of *dabuni*. He drew his sword and held it out in front of him horizontally. "All is fit and proper for the testing of this stranger for his worthiness to join the ranks of the *dabuni*. So let the fight begin." He raised the sword to the vertical and grasped it firmly with both hands.

Blade stood his ground, spear held in a guarding position. He wanted to let Jawai make the first move, revealing his style and perhaps weaknesses. But he knew that was more of a risk than usual now. Jawai's *katana*-style sword could kill or disable with a single blow. Its heavy blade, superb balance, and razor edge made it deadly. Blade knew that he had far less margin for error than usual, unless Jawai had some disastrously bad habit. But the odds were against Jawai's having reached his rank without being a first-class fighter.

Jawai took three steps forward, then stopped just out of range of any thrust from Blade. The sword seemed to freeze in his hands, as immobile and perfectly vertical as a stone pillar. Blade kept his eyes fixed on the sword. What mattered now was where it was, not where Jawai might be.

Then Jawai was coming in, taking a long, almost skipping step. The sword swung down from the vertical and flashed in the horizontal arc of a quick slash. Blade whipped his own spear over to the left, holding the guard position. In the same moment he leaped to the right, out of the path of the sword. The tip of the sword struck the spear with a sharp metallic *clink*. It was only the tip, but there was enough speed and weight behind it to make the spear shiver in Blade's hands. Definitely that sword could slice flesh and bone like a knife slicing paper. It might be able to chop through the spear shaft with a fair cut at full strength. Blade moved the spear back in front of his body and turned to face Jawai again.

Jawai came in again on the left, then a third time. Each time Blade leaped to one side, clearing the arc of the slash and warding off the sword with his spear.

Then Jawai came in a fourth time, suddenly shifting at the last second to the right.

But Blade had anticipated just exactly that change in the pattern. He sprang to the left, a long leap designed to take him completely clear of the arc of the sword. At the same moment he swung the spear down from the guard position to dart it out in a thrust at the captain's head. The razor-edged steel leaf darted within inches of Jawai's face. His eyes flared open in surprise and perhaps in a little fear as well. This time he stepped back farther and faster than before and watched Blade more intently. Blade took advantage of the delay to arrogantly twirl his spear around his head—keeping a firm grasp on the shaft with both hands, in case Jawai decided to move in suddenly.

Was Jawai perhaps assuming that Blade was an amateur who would fall easily when a serious attack came in? And in the meantime had he decided to just play with this stranger? That was almost too encouraging a thought, Blade realized. But if it was true, perhaps he should go on playing Jawai's game for a while.

There would be time enough to change the rules later, time enough to face the arrogant Captain Jawai with a game he had not expected to play.

The deadly dance around the square went on. Blade began to narrow his margin, judging and timing his leaps so that he was only inches clear of the deadly arc of Jawai's sword. Whether this leaping about was according to the standard rules for fighting in Gaikon, he didn't know. But Blade held a black belt in karate, and his footwork and endurance were formidable. The game Jawai had chosen for them to play was one Blade knew he could play for hours, if necessary.

It would probably be necessary. Blade quickly discovered that he would not be able to attack his opponent easily. Jawai was murderously fast on the riposte; Blade could not risk leaving himself open even briefly to deliver a serious attack.

After a while it began to seem as though they *had* been fighting for hours. Blade discovered that the captain telegraphed warning of overhead blows with a peculiar flexing of his wrists as he brought his sword up. Blade could easily respond to those signals in plenty of time to leap from under the downcuts. He didn't try to guard against them with his spear. They came down too hard and too fast for him to risk it. Too many blows with the tip might weaken his spear. A glancing blow might easily glance straight into his chest or thigh.

As he led Jawai in their dance around the square, Blade kept his eyes not only on the captain but also on the line of watching *dabuni* and on Yezjaro. He was looking for them to start reacting to what he was doing with Jawai. After only a few more minutes he saw that they were starting to react. And what he saw in their eyes was encouraging.

Obviously they understood more or less what he was doing. He saw men nodding or exchanging whispers with their companions. Yezjaro's face was almost expressionless, but Blade thought he saw faint hints of a smile on it. Obviously he was doing something right although he couldn't yet be sure exactly what it was. At least a *dabuno* of Gaikon did not have to simply stand up and hack away at an opponent and let the opponent hack back. He could properly use strategy and craft. That was fine with Blade. He knew he had no other hope of surviving here in this land of deadly swordsmen.

The wind rose further and blew colder and harder on Blade's face and across his bare chest. In spite of the cold and the wind, he was beginning to sweat.

Some of his muscles were also beginning to protest, particularly the legs that had already carried him so far so fast today.

But he could also see with growing pleasure that Jawai was getting tired, too, and was becoming confused. Perhaps Jawai had never fought so long before against such a strong opponent? Perhaps he had never expected to, and never developed the endurance he would need to last against Blade?

Certainly Jawai was no longer playing with Blade or trying to show off his expert swordwork. Each stroke of the sword lashed out like a flicker of flame, three feet of steel seeking Blade's life with all Jawai's strength and skill behind it. Blade realized one thing for certain about this fight: if he lost even a little bit of speed he was probably finished.

It was also obvious that the audience was becoming impatient. Blade couldn't tell which of the fighters was annoying them more, but he couldn't mistake the look of irritation on Yezjaro's face.

The fight went on. Except for the mounting roar of the wind, the thud of feet on chill wet grass, and the heavy breathing of the fighters, it went on in silence. Blade began to feel the muscles of his legs turning to white-hot bands stretched almost to the breaking point. He had to force his arms to twist and whirl the spear about as fast as before. And the red band around his head would no longer soak up all the sweat that was pouring down his face. He felt the stinging of salt in his eyes.

It was Yezjaro's voice that broke the silence. "What pleasure do you people find in this dance? Are you rehearsing a new act to present at the Hongshu's court during Lord Tsekuin's Journey of Obedience? I thought you came here to fight."

Blade knew that he was tired when he felt anger flare within him. But it flared only briefly. He recognized Yezjaro's tone of voice. For purposes of his own, the instructor was trying to push the fight to a conclusion by making one or the other of the fighters angry. Blade was determined that if there was going to be any anger and carelessness, it should be Jawai's.

Blade had guessed right. Jawai threw back his head and let out a high scream of rage and hatred. It seemed to be directed at the whole world, not just at Blade or Yezjaro. Then he came in, slashing with wild fury.

Blade leaped aside twice more as he judged distances and timing. He had known for a long time the perfect way to use the spear to end the fight. It was a way that would not only win but win with the style and flair he suspected the *dabuni* of Gaikon admired. But it was also risky. A split second off in the timing, and Blade knew that Jawai's sword would be slicing through his arm or into his thigh.

As Jawai came in for a third wild attack, Blade stood his ground. As Blade had expected, the captain slowed for a moment when he realized that his opponent was not leaping aside any more. That slowing and the captain's fatigue gave Blade all the time he needed. He dropped down into a crouch and lunged upward with the spear. One of the jutting hooks caught the descending sword. Blade sprang to his feet, twisting savagely as he did so. The sword flew out of Jawai's hands and high into the air, turning over and over as it flew. Before it thudded point-down into the soft earth, Blade had stepped back. The spear whirled around at full speed, and the butt smashed into the side of Jawai's neck. At the last moment Blade avoided smashing it into the captain's temple. He couldn't see any good reason for killing the man, if he could win his fight and the rank of *dabuno* without it.

Jawai was flung sideways by the blow and

sprawled facedown on the grass. Before he could make a move to rise, Blade was standing over him. One of Blade's feet came down on the small of Jawai's back, just hard enough to push him back down. His arms held the spear point-down over the back of Jawai's neck, ready to drive it down and in. Then he turned his head to look at Yezjaro and the house *dabuni*. His voice was cool but challenging as he spoke.

"Brother *dabuni*. Do you find me worthy to be among you?" He twirled the spear with an extra flourish, although his arms felt ready to drop off.

A long silence followed Blade's words, a silence in which it seemed that even the wind had faded away to listen. Blade looked at the silent figures standing and looking back at him, defiance written on his face and in every line of his athlete's body.

Again it was Yezjaro who broke the silence. "*I* say the stranger is worthy. I say it by my office as instructor to our clan. And I say it by my love of seeing a mighty and ingenious warrior." He grinned openly at Blade as he said the last words, and Blade grinned back. He had been right in his guess that in Gaikon they respected brains as well as brawn.

Now it was Yezjaro's turn to look a challenge at the house *dabuni*. "Brothers, will any of you say that the stranger is *not* worthy of the robe and the oil of Kunkoi?" He did not move his sword an inch. But the tone of voice he used could leave no one doubting what he would do to anyone who argued.

"It shall be as you wish," said one of the *dabuni*.

"Yes," said another. Then, with genuine enthusiasm that somewhat surprised Blade, "It will be an honor having him among us in the service of Lord Tsekuin."

Yezjaro's clipped voice cut the second man down to size. "It is too soon to say whether it will be an honor or not. But certainly it will not be improper nor displeasing to Kunkoi. I think we all agree on that." All the *dabuni* nodded. "Excellent." Then he turned to Blade.

"Stranger, you are judged fit to rank as a *dabuno* in the service of Lord Tsekuin. Is it your wish to do so?"

Blade realized that he knew next to nothing about Lord Tsekuin or what serving him might mean. But the service of a powerful warlord was a good enough place to start his exploration of this dimension. It might be one of those lands where a person without a lord was a person without status and with small chance of more than bare survival.

He nodded. "It is acceptable to me."

"Good," said Yezjaro. "You will take the oath when we reach the castle. We start tomorrow. One of these brothers will show you to a sleeping room."

Blade nodded. He was suddenly afraid to speak out loud, for fear that his voice would reveal how nearly exhausted he was.

The bedroom was small, but the walls were dark-colored and restful and gave off a faint scent. On the floor was a thick layer of bamboo mats and on top of that a straw-filled pad and a thick down-filled quilt. The pillows were made of leather, shaped like bars of pig iron and not much softer.

Two of the servant girls gave Blade a clean robe and led him to the bathhouse. There he soaked the chill and some of the aches out of himself while the girls sponged him down with pads of cloth soaked in scented oil, removing the last of the paint. They also kept pouring buckets of water into the tall wooden tub, keeping the water just below scalding temperature. When Blade finally climbed out of the tub and toweled himself off, he felt like a boiled lobster.

He took off the robe and crawled under the quilt. He had just decided to shove the pillows entirely aside when he heard footsteps approaching along the corridor outside. They stopped at the door. A moment later the sliding door scraped open, and a human figure showed in the opening, black against the light from outside.

Blade's training and instincts overcame his fatigue. In a single movement he rolled out of the quilt and off the pad. Then he sprang up, dropping into fighting stance as the visitor pulled the door shut and turned to look at him. He was about to snap out a challenge, when he recognized the visitor and laughed out loud.

It was Kika, the girl he had seen by the stream and in the kitchen. Now she stood by the door, wearing a pink robe with silver flowers embroidered across the breast. Her eyes ran up and down his body with obvious interest.

Blade laughed again and sat down on the quilt. "Well, young lady. What are you doing here now?"

The girl appeared to suddenly remember the respect owed to a *dabuno*. She dropped to her knees in a nervous flurry and bowed her head. "I am here to serve you, Honorable *Dabuno*. It was decided that my punishment for not taking care of the Honorable Instructor Yezjaro's robe should be to serve you this night."

Blade nodded. "Who decided this? Captain Jawai?"

The girl looked unmistakably startled. "Oh no, that could not be. It was the decision of the Honorable Instructor Yezjaro."

Blade nodded again. He understood or at least thought he understood more than he was probably supposed to. If Yezjaro was giving orders for punishing Captain Jawai's servants—that meant the captain was out of circulation, at least for tonight. With Yezjaro in charge, it was less likely that Blade would have to worry about a knife stuck into him in the darkness. That was a considerable relief.

The girl was young, but her body had unmistakably matured. Graceful curves were evident under the pink robe. And she gave off a subtle but undeniably appealing and arousing perfume. Blade suspected he knew the "service" she was supposed to render. Well, why not? He doubted if the *dabuni* were supposed to be ascetics. He certainly wasn't!

He remained standing, returning the girl's look, until she gave a little giggle and looked down at the floor. Without looking up, she undid the blue sash at her waist. The robe fell open. Then she shrugged slim shoulders, and the robe fell whispering to the floor and lay in a pink pool at her feet.

Like her perfume, the girl's beauty was subtle but arousing. All the curves were as delicate as if they had been drawn by a master artist with a very fine brush. In the dim light Blade could make out the faint sheen of shoulders and hips, the lift of small, pointed breasts with the nipples faint smudges at their tips, a small black strip almost perfectly centered between slim thighs. The girl threw her head back, until her black hair flowed down almost to the small of her back, and thrust her hips foward.

Yes, undeniably arousing. Blade couldn't have denied the arousal if he had wanted to. His massive member jutted forward, swollen, solid, sending urgent demands up to his brain. He responded to those demands. He stepped forward, lowered his massive hands until he could cup the girl's firm buttocks, and lifted her. Her eyes and mouth flared open as Blade drove upward between her legs, into her wet channel. Then she closed her eyes and stretched out her arms to grab Blade by the shoulders. Her legs twined around Blade's hips, locking her into place as she began to rock back and forth with Blade inside her.

She was not only wet but fantastically snug. After what seemed like only seconds Blade knew that she was going to push him over the edge soon. Too soon? He didn't know. He didn't know anything except that he needed and wanted to hold against the glorious agony that was boiling up in his groin and threatening to boil over. He didn't know anything, didn't care about anything, couldn't have paid attention to anything else if his life had depended on it. The girl was light, but his breath was coming in great sobbing gasps, and she seemed to be threatening to tear his aching arms out of their sockets as she twisted her hips around and around and around—

Suddenly she pressed down, locking herself so tightly around Blade that he felt as though the breath was being squeezed out of his body. But it was her breath that came out in a great shuddering gasping groan as she heaved herself up and down in a final desperate effort.

The girl's efforts put an end to Blade's self-control. His own hips twisted and turned as he felt his own heat spurting savagely upward into the girl, going on and on and on. There had been a terrible heat in him, and it took a long time for it all to be released.

But finally he was empty, and he lifted the half-conscious girl in his arms and laid her down on his sleeping pad. Then he lay down beside her and pulled the quilt over both of them.

As he finally drifted off to a deep sleep, Blade couldn't help running his mind back over his first day in Gaikon. A dangerous world, yes. But he suspected it would be a strangely exciting one as well.

7

Eight hours of sound sleep later, Blade awoke feeling ready to face whatever the land of Gaikon might throw at him. But it was another hour before a heavy-eyed Yezjaro appeared. Judging from the circles under his eyes and the look of satisfaction on his face, the instructor had spent most of the night in bed but not much of it sleeping.

There was no sign of Captain Jawai, and Blade decided not to ask about him. One of the house *dabuni* supervised the serving of breakfast, but his face was as expressionless as one of the mats on the floor.

After swallowing down the last of his soup and porridge, Yezjaro stood up, stretched, and looked down at Blade.

"There is no reason for us to delay our departure any more—brother. And there is also no reason for me not to call you by your war name. Have you one?"

"My name is Blade."

"Is that your war name or your house name?"

"In my homeland warriors have only a war name. It is a symbol of our dedication to war."

"A very great dedication indeed. But I am not surprised. Your warriors must be exceptionally devoted to developing their skills, if you are typical of them. Although you seem to emphasize speed more than precision, if your style is typical of your homeland."

"It is one style. We have many."

"As it is with us. We will have much to teach each other, I suspect. But *after* we reach the castle of Lord Tsekuin and you are sworn into his service." He began tying his sash and pulling on his sandals. "I have horses and traveling supplies ready for both of us, and my retainers are already mounted."

Blade decided to ask, "Are we going to say farewell to Captain Jawai? He was our host, after all, and—"

"The thought does you honor, Blade," said Yezjaro, with a faint smile. "But under the circumstances that ceremony would serve no purpose."

The party included six mounted retainers, one of them carrying a banner, and four pack horses. The rain had stopped by the time they rode out, and the sun was emerging from behind clouds. But a strong wind blew down a continuous spatter of drops as they rode on to the narrow path through the forest. Blade was raising a hand to wipe the water off his face when Yezjaro suddenly called out, "Stop!" and pointed off to the left.

"Blade, you were asking about Captain Jawai, I believe?"

Blade followed Yezjaro's outstretched arm, to a small clearing at the top of the slope beside the trail. On top of a thick pole sat the severed head of Captain Jawai. A little crust of dried blood had already covered the upper foot or two of the pole. The captain's bony features were set in a mask of grisly agony, and a few eager flies had already clustered around the staring eyes.

Blade urged his horse forward until he was alongside Yezjaro and spoke in a low voice so that only the instructor could hear. "Did you have it in mind for things to come out this way?" He jerked a thumb at the impaled head.

Yezjaro threw Blade the unmistakable look of a man not sure whether he should answer a question or not. But after a moment he replied in an equally soft voice, "Yes, I was hoping for it."

"May I ask why?"

"Quite simple. For many reasons the late Captain Jawai was unsuited for the post he held, particularly—" He broke off, hesitated, then began again. "He was unfit to protect the mines of Lord Tsekuin. But he would not resign. To have him dismissed or challenged and slain by one in Lord Tsekuin's service risked starting a feud within the ranks of the lord's own *dabuni*. This no wise man wished. It would give the Hongshu a great opportunity. But when I heard that a stranger who appeared warlike had come among us and already incurred the enmity of Jawai, I saw a clear path ahead."

Blade nodded. "Yes." His voice was deliberately cool. "If I slew Jawai or disgraced him so that he had to kill himself—"

"As he did."

"I thought so. If that happened, you would be rid of Jawai. And if he slew me, at least there would be none of my family or sworn friends determined to avenge me and disrupt the peace of Lord Tsekuin's household. A wise plan, if you have such great need of peace."

Yezjaro let the implied question pass him by. Instead he said, "You see clearly, Blade."

"When it is a question of my life or my honor, Yezjaro, I can see very far and listen very well. I ask you not to forget that."

Yezjaro nodded slowly. "I think I will take your advice, Blade." The party moved on down the trail.

It was a journey of three full days and part of a fourth to Lord Tsekuin's castle. It was a slow and tedious journey, most of it over trails that were always winding and sometimes steep and narrow. But the small, shaggy horses of Gaikon seemed to be nearly as tough and sure-footed as mountain goats. There were no accidents, not even when they had to lead the horses one at a time across a rope-and-plank bridge swaying dizzily a hundred feet above a mist-filled gorge.

During those days Blade learned a great deal about life in Gaikon. Much of the knowledge was essential, however many strange words it might contain. Some of it was unnecessary; Blade suspected Yezjaro of showing off his learning and boasting of his native land's virtues. That was a harmless and nearly universal game. Blade didn't say a word against it, not even when Yezjaro spent three hours reciting the epic poem of the Seven *Dabuni.*

But some of what Blade needed to know he had to pry out of Yezjaro like a pearl out of an oyster. There were a good many subjects about which the instructor remained as mute as a temple image.

In the land of Gaikon, one man reigned—the Emperor. Another man ruled—the Hongshu or Most Exalted Warlord. The country was divided into the Emperor's precincts, a number of cities directly under the Hongshu or the chancellors of his household, and the fiefs of a large number of greater or lesser warlords like Lord Tsekuin.

The members of the ruling families and households were something of a class apart, as were the warlords themselves. The rest of the people of Gaikon were divided into three broad categories: the warriors or *dabuni,* the merchants (who included the artisans), and the peasants. Blade was hardly surprised to learn that the *dabuni* considered themselves the source of all honor, virtue, and prowess in Gaikon, and that they despised and even abused the merchants and peasants. They were indeed like too many other warrior castes that Blade had met in too many other dimensions. But while he was in Gaikon, it was live by their rules or face a good chance of not living at all. And that meant learning as much as possible, whether Yezjaro told him willingly or not.

There was the time Yezjaro mentioned that the Most Exalted Warlord had the additional title of "Strong Younger Brother."

"How is that?" said Blade.

"In the tales of Kunkoi, the Sun Goddess, it is said she bore two sons, a year apart. The elder was terrible in his wisdom and magical powers, so he became the ancestor of our Emperors. The younger was far less wise, but he was the mightiest warrior since the beginning of time. He protected his brother's rule faithfully, and it is from him that the Hongshus claim their descent."

"I see," said Blade. Then he threw out a deliberately vague question. "This means, I take it, that the Hongshu is patron and master to the warlords of Gaikon?"

"Sometimes," said Yezjaro shortly.

"How can it be otherwise?" said Blade, trying to sound naive.

"It depends very much on the warlord," said Yezjaro. "Also on how honorable the Hongshu is. If a warlord has something the Hongshu covets—"

"I see," said Blade again. After a moment's remembering what he had heard at other times from the instructor, he thought he did see. "The Lord Tsekuin goes in some fear of inspiring the intervention of the Hongshu, doesn't he?"

"Perhaps." To Blade's trained ear, that short one-word reply was almost a shouted "Yes." He was silent for a moment, to give Yezjaro the impression that he had given up his questioning. Then:

"Does the Hongshu's interest in the affairs of Lord Tsekuin have something to do with mines? Possibly those mines that the late Honorable Captain Jawai was not fit to guard?"

Yezjaro said nothing. He didn't need to. The startled look on his face and then the quick masking of his expression told Blade more than enough.

There was another time when Blade and Yezjaro were sipping hot *saya* wine in the back room of a small tavern. They were discussing keeping the peace in the frequently turbulent and unruly families of the warlords.

"Often enough, it is decided to train the younger sons as scholars or send them into the service of Kunkoi," said the instructor. "Our own Lord Tsekuin was destined for a scholar's career. But Kunkoi's will was otherwise."

"How so?"

"The eldest son and heir died of a fever. So our Honorable Lord was called to put away his scrolls and brushes and his *Hu* board and take up steel."

"How well did he make the change?" asked Blade. He held out the flask of hot *saya*. The instructor practically snatched it from Blade's hand, poured his cup full, and drained it at a gulp. Then he leaned back, shaking his head slowly.

"Not as well as—" He broke off and shot a hard look at Blade. "He is young yet, and has much to learn. He will learn it, I am sure."

Blade sensed that Yezjaro's suspicions might be aroused if he pushed any farther. But he also sensed he might be on the brink of learning something important.

So he gambled. "You're a strange one to call a warlord 'young,'" said Blade. He managed to put laughter into his voice. "Unless he's hardly more than a child. You can't be much more than—"

"I'm ten times older than Lord Tsekuin is in what counts now!" snarled Yezjaro. "He's thirty, I know.

But he didn't pick up a sword at six, or kill his first man at twelve, or fight in a pitched battle at fourteen and live through it! And he didn't put on the blue robe at sixteen! I did. So if I want to think he's young, Kunkoi knows I've got the right to!" He poured himself more *saya*, and gulped it down.

Blade dropped the topic. He didn't want to push things any farther. Certainly not to the point of provoking the instructor to a fight. Blade suspected that was a fight he would lose. Even if by some chance he won, he would lose a strong and useful guide and ally.

In spite of occasional bits of luck like this, Blade did not learn as much as he wanted to on the journey. He certainly learned enough to know that he would have to be careful. His eyes would have to be looking in all directions at once, his hand ready to snatch up a spear, and his feet as ready as a cat's to jump.

But that he would have known without exchanging a single word with anyone. It was the only way of staying alive in Dimension X.

8

Late in the morning of the fourth day they rode out of the forest into the fields around the castle of Lord Tsekuin.

Yezjaro had sent a messenger on ahead to bring word to the castle. So Blade was not surprised to see the farmers, who had been working knee-deep in the flooded paddy fields, crowding up to the edge of the road as the party rode past. He was only slightly surprised at the open smiles, the cheers, and the ribald remarks that greeted the young swordsman. Yezjaro, for all his swashbuckling arrogance, was obviously popular.

They rode past paddy fields and villages of thatched wooden houses for nearly an hour. Then Blade saw a sprawling tangle of towers, buildings, and walls crowning a high hill about three miles ahead. He didn't need Yezjaro's comment to realize that they were approaching the castle. Nor did he need the instructor's pointing hand to notice the cluster of banners gliding out of the gate and moving swiftly down the hill toward them.

"As I hoped, the Lord Tsekuin himself is coming out to greet us. That is good news for you, Blade. If the lord is prepared to admit in public that you have rendered him a valuable service—well, you may find yourself in a stronger position than I had expected.

But do not buy the barrels for *saya* made from grain as yet unharvested."

"We have such sayings and rules in my own land, Yezjaro," said Blade, deliberately showing more irritation than he felt. "As I have told you, I can see more than a small child and hardly like being treated as one."

"So shall it be," said Yezjaro, with a small bow and a large grin. Both held a hint of mockery. Then the instructor was reining in his horse and signaling the rest of the party to do the same. They pulled up to a stop in the road, and waited while the cluster of banners came bobbing and waving toward them.

The man who was obviously Lord Tsekuin was spurring along well ahead of his men. Blade had an extra chance to observe him as he rode up. The warlord was certainly no child. In fact, he must have been on the wrong side of thirty. But there was a softness about his face and his lanky figure that suggested he was still more accustomed to chairs and scrolls than to saddles and swords. Although he was riding out in front of his escort at a good clip, he was obviously not doing it because he felt comfortable on a fast-moving horse.

With much sawing on the reins the warlord brought his horse to a stop in front of Blade and Yezjaro. Blade noticed that he nearly went headfirst out of the saddle as the horse stopped. Yezjaro removed his broad leather hat and bowed from the waist. Blade did the same.

"Welcome home, Worthy Instructor Yezjaro," said Lord Tsekuin. "And welcome, *dabuno* Blade. I understand it is your wish to enter my service?"

"It is, Honorable Lord Tsekuin," said Blade.

"That is good. Our house has need of strong *dabuni*, and many such rise high." The warlord's voice was clear but high-pitched. He put no force and no sincerity that Blade could detect into the formal greetings. Perhaps he didn't feel any? There was nothing to do about it if he didn't. Besides, there was something else about Lord Tsekuin that practically jumped out at Blade and slapped him in the face.

The warlord positively dripped diamonds. Blade saw small ones in rings on three fingers of each hand and others set in a large circular gold pin that held his sash together. Slightly larger ones flashed from a medallion on a chain around his neck and from a badge on the front of his hat. A huge one—a good forty carats of the finest gem quality—flashed from the hilt of his sword.

As the warlord's escort rode up Blade noticed that they too were decked out with a princely abundance of diamonds. Not quite on the scale of their lord, of course. No doubt those forty-carat monsters didn't grow on bushes even in Gaikon. But all had at least one piece of diamond-studded jewelry and a jeweled sword-hilt.

Blade realized that he didn't need to ask what Lord Tsekuin's mines produced. Nor did he need to wonder why the Hongshu might be intriguing against Lord Tsekuin and casting greedy eyes on his lands.

He also realized that Yezjaro and Tsekuin had been exchanging polite formalities while he stared at the warlord. Now both broke off suddenly and looked back along the road toward the castle.

A large red two-wheeled cart was rumbling toward them, drawn by four horses and carrying a tented enclosure perched behind the two drivers. Blade saw both Yezjaro and Lord Tsekuin grimace. The warlord's escort reluctantly made a clear path for the cart. With shouts and whip-cracking it came to a stop just behind Lord Tsekuin's horse. The green curtains were thrust open from within, and a woman's head peered out.

The woman wore a narrow mask of red leather over her eyes, and black silk gloves. She wore no jewels on her fingers or clothes. But these were her only concessions to the public modesty that custom required of noblewomen in Gaikon. Around her slender, creamy brown throat and in her black hair she wore enough diamonds to stock a fair-sized home dimension jeweler's store. The eyes that stared out through the large holes in the mask did not drop to the ground when Blade met that stare. They held his own eyes, openly, frankly, almost appraisingly. Then the initial boldness in the woman's eyes faded. Blade sensed something admiring and almost welcoming in them. He felt it so strongly and unmistakably that he wondered how Lord Tsekuin could avoid noticing it.

Whatever Lord Tsekuin noticed, it was enough to set off his temper. His eyes flared as he saw the woman peering out of her cart. His voice rose to a screech.

"Back to the castle, Lady! You shame the house, out here. Back, I say!" If the glare on his face had been turned into heat, the lady, cart, horses, and drivers would have all vanished in a puff of smoke.

The lady at least had enough sense not to argue. The curtains closed behind her as the two drivers began struggling with reins and whips to get the cart turned around. Lord Tsekuin did not help matters by storming at them with shrill curses and snapping his own riding whip at the heads of the horses. But finally they clattered off toward the castle, followed by a good many stares—including Blade's.

Lord Tsekuin turned back to Yezjaro and Blade, his voice still hoarse and shaking from his burst of rage. "I am shamed for this befouling of your welcoming, worthy brothers. But I—" He threw up his hands in a gesture of disgust and despair, turned his own horse, and cantered off after the cart. His escort followed in disorderly haste.

When the last of them was out of earshot, Blade turned to Yezjaro. "The woman in the cart—that was the Lady Oyasa, wasn't it?"

"Do you think there is great wisdom in realizing that, Blade?"

"No, I think there is only the ability to see what is in front of one's eyes. And that ability I told you I have."

"True. But there are times when a blind man may reach a higher level of wisdom than one who sees clearly."

"No doubt there are such times. But is this one of them? Or is it a question of merely a longer life, rather than a higher level of wisdom?"

"You place so little value on life, Blade?"

"That is a question that must be answered each time one's life is in danger. If there was one answer and only one, all warriors would either die young or live to a great age."

Yezjaro threw back his head and laughed. "Blade, if you spend enough time in Gaikon, I can conceive that your sayings will fill many scrolls, like the war words of the great *dabuno* Mino Tojai. You speak like a man both brave and wise. I hope your wisdom will make it possible for your bravery to receive the honors it deserves."

Blade rather hoped so too. But there was certainly a nasty mixture of elements here in the fief of Lord Tsekuin. A young, hot tempered, and petulant lord, ill-suited to his rank and position. Diamonds that apparently could be scooped out of the ground as easily as potatoes out of a backyard garden. A strong-willed lady with a sharp eye and little wish to bow to the customs of Gaikon that governed other ladies of her rank. And hovering over them all, a greedy Hongshu who understandably lusted after that openly flaunted wealth of jewels.

9

The next day Blade was sworn into the service of Lord Tsekuin. He received a blue robe embroidered with the gold sun and the clan badge of Tsekuin-La, two swords and a spear from the armory, and an annointing with the sacred oil of Kunkoi. Judging from the smell of the oil, it had been around nearly since the time of the Sun Goddess' last appearance in Gaikon some three thousand years before. Blade could smell it thirty yards upwind. After the castle's ninety-year old priestess of Kunkoi had rubbed the oil on Blade's arms and into his pubic hair, everyone could smell *him* thirty yards upwind.

Fortunately, Gaikon was a dimension in which people could and did take regular baths, with hot water and soap.

Blade settled in to learning what was required of a house *dabuno* in the service of Lord Tsekuin. Fortunately, he already knew or could guess most of it. As a lesser brother among the *dabuni* (with his temples and a strip over the top of his skull shaved), he had to sit well to the rear, look sharp, be obedient, and keep his mouth shut. That was the best possible way of learning things, anyway.

Except for the use of the distinctive curved sword, Blade already knew most of the *dabuno's* standard weapons. He took to the bow in particular with spectacular skill. The archery instructor might turn as white as a starched bedsheet at Blade's lack of "philosophy" in his archery. But the more practical among the *dabuni* pointed out that even without philosophy Blade could put eight successive arrows into a six-inch circle at four hundred yards, with the last one on its way before the first one had hit.

"Therefore," as Yezjaro put it, "he may be forgiven having come to our philosophy somewhat late in life. Are there any who dispute this?"

There was very seldom anybody who disputed anything with Yezjaro, a notable advantage for Blade. Their friendship was further cemented when the instructor took personal charge of teaching Blade how to use the deadly sword of Gaikon. After several weeks of exercises each day, Blade knew he was a long way from being a finished swordsman by Gaikon's standards.

"I fear that at least a third of the swordsmen you would meet could now slice you up like a fisherman slicing salt bait," said Yezjaro one afternoon. "So pick your quarrels with the other two-thirds for the moment. You have both the body and the soul of a warrior, however. It will not be long before you can take on all but a few of Gaikon's swordsmen and walk away."

"How long is 'not long'?" asked Blade, with a grin.

"Oh, not more than four years," said Yezjaro. "But do not despair. Even now there are not a dozen men I have met who could touch you with a spear. I know I could not. And your skill with the bow is all but something out of a legend. Any *dabuno* who thinks you are a helpless babe is unlikely to live long. But if you are wise and learn well, you will live long and die in your bed with your wives, concubines, numerous descendants, and a still more numerous household lamenting your passing into the arms of Kunkoi."

"Then let us go and drink to dying in bed," said Blade. "Though obviously bed must be the most dangerous place in the world, considering how many people die there."

It was a hoary joke in Home Dimension, but it made Yezjaro laugh all the way to the cellar where the hot *saya* awaited them.

Blade saw no more of Lady Oyasa as time passed. Except when the whim took her, she apparently stayed in proper seclusion in the women's wing of the sprawling castle. The approaches to that wing were guarded by booby traps (or so Yezjaro said), by a contingent of six-foot eunuchs, and by several of Lady Oyasa's personal maids who had taken training in arms.

Yezjaro pointed out one of them as the one person in the whole castle who probably knew the most about the affairs of the warlord and his family. He also warned Blade against trifling with her.

Blade hardly needed the warning. Lady Musura was not unattractive, although rather gaunt and well into her thirties. But she sported a collection of scars on the right side of her face, and normally carried at least two knives in her sash. She was reputed to have been—when younger—a *jinai,* one of the sworn order of assassins and secret agents serving the Hongshu. When these grew too old, some retired to the special secluded villages maintained by the *jinai* clans. Others renounced safety and seclusion and remained in the outer world. Only a few took service with warlords, but even those who did always remained to some degree their own masters.

Certainly Blade could not imagine anyone getting from Lady Musura a loyalty she was not willing to give. Always taciturn, seldom smiling, the only time she apparently cared to speak to Blade was when they were on the archery range. Although her lighter bow could not carry as far as Blade's seven-footer, she could match his shooting within the range of about two hundred yards.

It was not much of a bond between them, but it was one that enabled two otherwise different people to talk to each other. Both were experts in the skills of a warrior, and both turned out to have an equally keen eye for intrigue and conspiracy.

This also meant that Blade learned more about the situation facing Lord Tsekuin than Yezjaro had ever cared to tell him. As much as people tried to keep their worries off their faces and out of their conversation, no one in the castle had much real hope for peace. That the Hongshu would move against Lord Tsekuin sooner or later was more or less assumed. Lady Musura suspected that the move might take place during the forthcoming Journey of Obedience to the Hongshu's capital.

"The Journey must be made once every four years," she said. "Four years ago our lord's father was alive, and the Hongshu respected him enough to deal justly with him, for all his growing wealth. And the eldest son was also alive then, a formidable warrior. But now both are gone. You have seen the man who now rules this fief as the Lord Tsekuin. Are you surprised that the Hongshu thinks he may be easily separated from his great and growing wealth?"

"Not at all," said Blade. "I am surprised that he has waited so long."

"The Journey of Obedience is the best occasion," said Lady Musura. "Lord Tsekuin will be in the Hongshu's capital, ignorant of the etiquette of the court, with only a small retinue of picked warriors. He will never be more at the mercy of the Hongshu and his various chancellors, who have even more greed and fewer scruples than the Hongshu himself." She hesitated before going on. "Perhaps he has also been waiting to be sure that the emperor will not interfere. But I doubt that."

"Why? Is the emperor that helpless?"

"To some degree, yes. There have been emperors with the skills to make their 'strong younger brothers' walk a straight path in dealing with loyal warlords. But he who sits upon the Sun Throne today—" Her voice trailed off.

Blade finished the sentence mentally. A weak or self-indulgent emperor, a strong and unscrupulous Hongshu, and a foolish, headstrong, and ill-informed warlord. Those who were predicting trouble during the Journey of Obedience seemed to be making sense.

10

Gaikon's year moved on toward spring. The snow melted on the mountains to the west, swelling buds made the trees a green haze on the hills, the farmers worked late in their paddies setting in the fresh shoots. Winter clothing and winter quilts were stored away one by one. Yezjaro moved his sword practice with Blade out into one of the courtyards.

The year was also moving toward the Journey of Obedience. People no longer made any particular effort to hide their concern about it, although they said more to Blade with their faces than with their lips. Only Lady Musura continued to speak freely. Blade found himself more than willing to join the hunts that Yezjaro and other senior *dabuni* organized in the forests that lay between the castle and the mountains. Like them, he needed something to take his mind off the approaching crisis.

The morning of his fourth hunt, Blade awoke to find an arrow sticking in the wall above his head. It had obviously been fired in through the narrow latticed window during the night. Blade did not need the letter that was tied around the arrow to know that it could only have been fired by Lady Musura. No one else in the castle could have hit the narrow window from the nearest place that offered a clear shot, a good hundred and fifty yards away.

The note said:

"I will speak to you with another arrow today while you ride on the hunt. Ride so that none may overhear."

Blade couldn't help wondering what Lady Musura had in mind for him if he followed her request—and what she had in mind for him if he didn't. But if she felt he was dangerous, she could and would pick him off when and where she chose. Besides, his curiosity was aroused. So he decided to watch for her arrow and then "listen" to what it might say to him.

It bothered no one when Blade asked to ride in the rear of the hunting party. Except for Yezjaro and Doifuzan, the gray-haired first *dabuno* of Lord Tsekuin, most of the warriors of the castle found Blade a little hard to understand or accept. Therefore they never objected when he chose to remain a little apart.

The six hunters rode in silence for several miles, then dismounted to cross a shallow river by a ford marked by two large yellow-barked trees growing side by side on the opposite bank. Blade was just stopping his horse to remount on the far side when he heard a faint *whuffff* overhead and a slightly louder *chunk.* He recognized the sound of one of Lady Musura's special silent *jinai* arrows, and looked up. The arrow was sticking into the right-hand tree about three feet above Blade's head. He swung up into the saddle, waited until the last of the other hunters was out of sight ahead, then stood in his stirrups and pulled down the arrow.

The paper around this one read:

"At sunset, the arrow's feathers bid you to the correct path."

Blade looked along the direction from which the arrow had come. The "correct path" led straight downstream for about a hundred yards, then vanished into the forest again. When he had memorized the direction, he urged his horse forward to catch up with the rest of the hunting party.

The day's hunting was for wild mountain sheep, elusive game that more often than not led their hunters a merry chase over mile after mile of countryside. So Blade only had to be a little "careless" in keeping track of his fellow hunters in order to find himself alone as the sun began to sink toward the horizon. By the time it had dipped to the treetops, he was back at the ford.

Blade dismounted and led his horse along the bank of the stream until the forest began to close about him. Then he found a concealed place to tether the horse, took his spears, and struck off into the trees.

It was heavy going. The shadows were already thick and the heavy underbrush made it difficult to keep on course. Blade could not help wondering about his chances of getting anywhere in this unknown forest after darkness came down. He had the feeling that he might wind up getting lost. That wouldn't be dangerous, but it would be embarrassing.

On the other hand it might be dangerous after all. Nerves were growing tighter and tighter in the castle. His absence might be hard to convincingly explain. Suppose Lord Tsekuin came to suspect that Blade had been out in the forest meeting with agents of the Hongshu?

Before Blade could consider any more unpleasant possibilities, he saw ruddy sunset light shining through the trees ahead. A few more steps, and Blade saw a small clearing with a tumbledown hut, obviously long abandoned. On the roof of the hut lay a small figure dressed in black. Blade recognized Lady Musura, wearing the black costume of a *jinai* without the hood and mask.

He stayed under cover, though, until he had examined the forest around the clearing almost tree by tree and bush by bush. He trusted that Lady Musura had some good reason for wanting him here. But he realized he still did not know enough about life in Gaikon to completely rule out treachery.

There seemed to be nothing in the forest within sight or hearing except a swelling chorus of insects. Blade unslung his spear and held it in one hand as he stepped out of cover, then raised it in salute. Lady Musura sprang to her feet, raised one hand in greeting, and pointed downward with the other. She seemed to be pointing toward the door of the hut. Blade saw that the gap between the sagging door and the frame had been largely sealed with strips of red leather.

The color and the material struck sparks in Blade's memory. Lady Oyasa and her red leather mask, the day she had come out to inspect the new *dabuno!* Blade froze almost in midstride, then glared up at Lady Musura. The black-clad *jinai* woman returned his glare with a bland smile—then nocked an arrow to her bow and pointed it at Blade. Blade measured the distance to the hut and the cover of the forest. It would be a miracle if he could make it to the forest safely, but to the hut—

Without any tensing of muscles to warn the sharp-eyed woman, Blade sprang forward. He covered the twenty feet to the hut in two tremendous leaps, stopping just below her. The lady crouched on the edge of the overhanging roof, turning to bring her bow to aim at Blade. Before she could draw a bead on him he thrust upward with his spear. The spearhead shot up between the bow and the bowstring. Then Blade swung the spear outward with all his strength and weight behind it.

In her surprise at Blade's attack, Lady Musura was a fraction of a second slow in letting go of her bow.

The spear jerked the bow savagely outward and she followed it, to the edge of the roof and over.

She was still in midair as Blade jerked the spear back, sending the bow flying out into the field. Then he reversed the spear, striking with the butt and shaft at Lady Musura as she landed. With the catlike quickness of the trained *jinai,* the lady flipped in midair to land on her feet. But once again she was a fraction of a second too slow to cope with Blade. His thrust with the butt end of the spear caught her in the stomach. She gasped and started to double over. Then he swung the spear shaft sideways and caught her behind the knees. She went down, and Blade reversed the spear again, closed in, and stood over her with the point of the spear at her throat.

Then he laughed. "Lady Musura, I hope you'll believe me when I say that I don't have any quarrel with you. So I wouldn't like to kill you. Also, killing you would weaken the forces of Lord Tsekuin, to whom I have sworn an oath, at a time when he must be as strong as possible. But I could kill you if I wanted to. You admit that?"

From somewhere Lady Musura managed to drag out one of her rare smiles. But there was also sincere respect in her voice as she said, "I do admit it. I would stand little chance against you unless I caught you by surprise, and then I might at best die beside you. A *jinai* of your size and strength at the height of his power and training would no doubt do a better job. But even he would find himself with a fight to remember, if he won."

"I thank you for the praise, Lady Musura. But you have not said if you will answer my questions."

"I can make no promises when I do not know the questions, Blade. Is it strange to you that there are things I would rather die by slow torture than speak of to you?"

"It is not," admitted Blade. "Very well. Who is inside that hut? And why are they here, and why are you guarding them?"

The woman on the ground smiled more broadly. "If you had not been so afraid of traps, Blade, you would have found answers to those questions by now. The answers lie there—" She pointed at the door with the red leather.

"I never fear traps unless I'm made to suspect them," said Blade sharply. "But having arrows pointed at me for no good reason makes me suspect traps and treachery. There is so much of it in the air now."

The lady jerked her head, acknowledging that Blade had a point. Then her face softened. "Blade, go through that door—I ask you as an honorable comrade and *dabuno*. Go through that door, and if you keep silence and show discretion, no harm shall come to you or anyone else."

Blade detected sincerity in her voice—enough to make him relax somewhat, not enough to make him shift the spear. "Do you swear by Kunkoi and by your honor as a *jinai*?"

"By these I swear, Blade," said Lady Musura. "And I will gladly swear by any of the gods of your own land that will accept my oath." There was an unfamiliar note in her voice, almost a pleading one.

"Well, then," said Blade, raising the spear. He had turned away before Lady Musura could say anything to thank him.

Inside the hut the light was dim and ruddy, but it was strong enough for Blade to see that the place had recently been swept free of dust and cobwebs. The air was close and thick, in contrast to the fresh coolness of the evening outside. It was heavy with the smells of dust, dry rot, incense, and perfume.

Perfume? Blade looked more closely and realized

that the far end of the hut had been partitioned off with dark red curtains hung from the ceiling. Through the crack under the curtains Blade saw the faint orange yellow glow of lamplight. Then he saw the curtains move slightly, as though pushed from behind, and heard a deep-throated woman's laugh.

"What are you waiting for, Blade? I heard Lady Musura promising you safety. Do you doubt her word?"

Blade could not have stopped more suddenly if a bear trap had clamped itself on his leg. The voice belonged to Lady Oyasa.

Blade's wits did not stop, however. His voice was cool as he replied, "I do not doubt her word, Honorable Lady. But I—"

"Then why do you stand there?" There was an imperious note in that question. This was a young woman accustomed to getting answers to her questions, whether they made any sense or not.

"I doubt the wisdom of my being here in this hut with you at this hour and no one else present," said Blade sharply. "I will say nothing out of loyalty to Lord Tsekuin. But I will say something about folly that could bring us both under the executioner's sword—if we were granted such a merciful death. And what of the Hongshu? Would you throw him a perfect excuse to intervene in your husband's affairs, with Kunkoi alone knows what consequences?"

A hiss of indrawn breath followed Blade's words, and after that came a long silence. Blade heard the rustle of garments and the scrape of sandals on the floor as Lady Oyasa shifted position, but still she made no answer. He waited in silence, his eyes occasionally flickering toward the door. It was the lady's move now, if she chose to make it.

He rather hoped she would have the sense not to.

"Blade," she said finally. "Come behind the curtains

and sit down. I see that you speak from a wisdom that I once had. But no more. I am not afraid of folly. I beg of you—come and listen to me, at least." There was no mistaking the tone in her voice. She was begging now, not commanding. She sounded almost desperate.

Blade shrugged and stepped forward. A woman who demanded or threatened—that he could refuse and had refused. It was one reason why he was still alive. But a woman who begged made an appeal he had to answer.

Lady Oyasa sat behind the curtain at the head of a long double sleeping pad, with several folded quilts stacked at the foot. She wore a robe the same color as the flame of the lamp, with a circlet of small diamonds set in gold around her unbound black hair. Her face was not only unmasked but free of any cosmetics. Blade was surprised at how young she now seemed—no more than twenty.

He made a ceremonial bow, and saw a grimace pass across her face. One hand clenched around a fold of her robe. "Blade, I beg you also—no ceremony. Do you have any idea of how tired one can become of ceremony? No, I do not imagine you have been in Gaikon long enough to see all the horrors our etiquette can inflict on one who must live with it always. And when one is married to a man—" She hesitated, then her courage returned and her words came out in a rush. "When one is married to a man one saw for the first time the day of the wedding, who makes even the few times he comes to one's bed a ceremony, who has the skills of a scholar but the temper of a spoiled boy—Kunkoi has sent enough already. One should not have to endure more."

"But one does, Honorable Lady," said Blade.

The lady shook her head and smiled. "Not tonight, Blade. Not tonight, not here, and not between us."

Blade had barely recognized the suppressed desire in her voice when she stood up and came toward him. She moved with long free strides, not with the normal half-shuffle of noblewomen in Gaikon. As she moved, her hands went to the diamond-studded clasp that held together the sash of her robe. The sash dropped to the floor. The robe did not follow it, but it swung open and shut as Lady Oyasa covered the last few steps to Blade. He could see the flicker of slim, rounded, creamy brown limbs inside the robe.

Then Lady Oyasa was flowing up against him, her hands working on his own robe, working up under it. He was responding, and he knew it, and he knew that she knew it. She laughed and murmured, her lips pressed against his throat. "I thought you were no eunuch, Blade. Now I know. It would be a pity for someone like you not to be a man."

It certainly would be, Blade thought. He knew that castration was one of the penalties for what he was about to do. But he was going to do it anyway. Lady Oyasa was right. There was a time for worrying about what was foolish and what wasn't, and a time for throwing caution to the winds. He reached down and wrapped his arms around Lady Oyasa, drawing her more tightly against him.

She was tall for a woman of Gaikon, tall and long-limbed. She could run her fingers through his hair without reaching, press her warm lips against his throat and run them up and down the side of his neck. She twisted from side to side as she did this, and bit by bit the robe crept wider and wider open. Then suddenly with a faint hiss of silk on soft skin it was gone, falling and spreading on the sleeping mat at her feet. Her whole exquisite body gleamed bare, the highlights shifting as she slowly turned about in front of Blade.

Then suddenly she knelt down and after a moment

almost threw herself backward. "Oh, Blade," she murmured. "Let it be now. Let it be now, and not a moment later. It is time for us. Kunkoi would have it so." Slowly her legs spread apart, inch by inch, as she spoke. Meanwhile her hands cupped her small conical breasts, whose nipples were already solidly erect spots of darkness against the creamy brown skin.

If Blade hadn't already decided to answer Lady Oyasa's appeal, he would have decided at that moment. He was not a stone statue, and nothing else could have resisted the appeal of Lady Oyasa's naked body—and the naked desire in her eyes and voice. His hands worked swiftly, stripping off his own robe, then he lay down on the mat beside her.

His hands roamed up and down her body, while her hands did the same on his. She nuzzled his throat again, and nipped the tanned skin with small sharp white teeth. Desire swelled further in Blade, a desire to lose himself in this woman, to lock his arms around her. He had not felt such a total desire for a long time; he had wondered if it was perhaps something he had lost.

But it was not, and so he gave into it. He pulled Lady Oyasa over on top of him, and she settled down to take him into herself, deep and deeper, until they were locked together more tightly than Blade would have imagined possible. His arms bent her downward even farther, until her gorged and solid nipples brushed his chest. Her flesh was both cool and hot at the same time. Its feel against his own drove Blade's desire higher—higher and faster even than the tightness and wetness and warmth that were wrapped around him.

Lady Oyasa began grinding her hips down against Blade, twisting them around in a circle, rocking her body from side to side against his chest. She began to whimper, then to gasp in a rhythm that increased to match Blade's. Her long fingers arched themselves into claws and raked through his hair, digging into his scalp. But the pain did not penetrate Blade's mind. Nothing did, nothing could. He was becoming totally absorbed in this woman, in the act of love with her. No, not necessarily love, or even affection. Passion—raw, burning, and exhilarating enough in its own right.

Suddenly Lady Oyasa's fingers clamped down hard, her nails digging deep into Blade's scalp. He gasped with the sudden stabbing pain and his efforts to hold on. She opened her mouth wide and let out a howl of pure animal feeling, a howl that filled the hut. It was so loud Blade could imagine it escaping through the walls and being carried for miles through the forest outside. The lady thrashed and heaved and twisted as though an electric shock was passing through her, alternately jerking half upright and plastering herself harder than ever against Blade.

Then Blade himself groaned and let out a shout of relief and triumph as his own spasm came. It was his turn to lock his arms around Lady Oyasa, his turn to run his fingers through her hair, his turn to pull her hard against him as he jetted furiously up into her still-twisting body. For long minutes they stayed locked together in a common release, and if the hut had fallen in on them they would not have noticed it.

Eventually the explosion of passion faded away. Blade lay on the mat, one arm curled around Lady Oyasa, waiting for his breathing to return to normal, feeling his body as damp with sweat as it would have been after a battle. Even after he had the breath to do so, he did not feel like speaking.

Lady Oyasa broke the silence, propping herself up on one elbow and looking down at Blade with a soft smile on her face. Even now Blade could not help noticing that her breasts were so firm they did not sag or droop out of shape as she took this ungraceful pose. She ran the tip of one finger lightly across Blade's rib cage and said, "Well, Blade—what of folly now?"

Blade shrugged. "I think I will not try to judge folly for you, Lady. You seem to follow your own judgment and no one else's."

"How well you know me," she said with a laugh. "How much better than Lord Tsekuin. Yes, I do follow my own judgment. And look where it has led me. Now I will not have to submit to a widow's seclusion at twenty-one without ever having known real pleasure."

"It may yet lead you farther than you wish to go," said Blade, trying to keep his voice light.

"Perhaps," she said. "But I have only one head to cut off. I have only one body they can torture, one back they can flog. I can lose only so much to Lord Tsekuin's whims."

Blade had to admit that she was right. But he did not share her casualness about *his* "one head" or "one body." What there was between them had been marvelous and might be so again. But he could hardly share Lady Oyasa's notion that it was worth so much.

11

Blade and Lady Oyasa met in the forest hut three more times during the next three weeks. They might have done it more often if they had risked meeting in the castle itself. But that would have meant disarming too many booby traps and bribing too many guards and servants to keep eyes, ears, and mouths shut. Sooner or later word would have reached Lord Tsekuin.

Then there would have been less than no chance of mercy for them. Lord Tsekuin was in a foul mood these days. He walked about with a hand on the hilt of his sword and his eyes constantly roving about him, even in the castle. He looked like he expected six armed opponents to leap at him out of the walls or sprout up around him from the ground under his feet.

Meanwhile there was weapons practice. There was instruction in all the manners and skills of a *dabuno*, including the approved games such as *Hu*. Blade did not find time heavy on his hands.

Blade's swordsmanship steadily improved under Yezjaro's teaching. It improved to the point where Yezjaro admitted, "It might take me as much as ten minutes to kill you, Blade." That was high praise from the deadly young instructor.

In spear fighting there was no one in the castle who could last more than a couple of minutes with Blade. Yezjaro himself said, "If you were not a wandering stranger, I would have you made an instructor in the spear, under me. But it is too soon yet to expect most of our *dabuni* to obey you properly. After we return from the Journey of Obedience, there may be time for you to gain the respect you deserve."

"*If* we return from the Journey of Obedience," said Blade grimly. "Or if we do not return with more important things to deal with than my status."

Yezjaro returned Blade's smile. "So our worries are becoming yours?"

"Why not? I have sworn an oath and I am not without notions of honor. Besides, a man can breathe in fear from the air of this castle."

Yezjaro's smile faded. He did not like to hear the word "fear" mentioned when speaking of warriors. But at least he was not one of those thick-headed *dabuni* who would have challenged Blade on the spot for saying the word. He had too much sense for that—and he was too aware of how serious the situation was.

The time for the Journey of Obedience approached rapidly. The matter came up of choosing the forty *dabuni* who would accompany Lord Tsekuin on the Journey. A good many of the house *dabuni* would have been happy to have Blade stay behind.

"But don't worry about that," Yezjaro told him. "I know that Doifuzan and I see alike on this. Being part of the Journey of Obedience will be an important part of your training as a *dabuno*. You will learn much through seeing the court of the Hongshu with your own eyes. Indeed, I think I could talk until Kunkoi's chimes sound for the next Season of the World without telling you as much as your own eyes will."

Yezjaro and Doifuzan both spoke out for Blade, and Lord Tsekuin followed their advice. He usually did. With their lord choosing Blade to accompany him, none of the *dabuni* could properly do more than mutter into their wine cups and glower at Blade.

Blade was too happy about being able to join the Journey of Obedience to worry about the other *dabuni*. The more he saw of Gaikon, the better he would be carrying out his mission of exploring new dimensions. In any case, he had never liked sitting it out while things happened somewhere else. It didn't make any difference how dangerous those things might be. Blade was a natural adventurer, born into the wrong century for that kind of man—the twentieth century of large institutions and organization men. But Project Dimension X had given him the perfect job.

Lord Tsekuin would be taking forty *dabuni* with him on the Journey of Obedience, as well as servants, porters, cooks, and messengers. These would accompany the party to Deyun, the Hongshu's capital. But they would not enter the Hongshu's palace. "No one but a *dabuno* or a person under the sponsorship and protection of one may enter the palace," said Yezjaro.

"I suppose the Hongshu feels that a *dabuno's* sense of honor makes him less—dangerous?"

"Quite right. For a mere breach of etiquette a *dabuno* can be asked to commit suicide—and he will. That is also why the etiquette is so strict and so complex. It will tangle the feet, the tongues, and the swords of any who have not had it hammered into their skulls for many years.

"That is one reason why I fear for Lord Tsekuin's fate in Deyun. During the years when he was destined for scholarship, he learned much, but not court etiquette. He has had little time and less desire to learn since his succession."

"I see," said Blade.

"I hope so," said Yezjaro grimly. "I would not have

you, whom I have sponsored personally, disgrace the clan by any breach of etiquette. For the clan there might be mercy, if the Hongshu is willing to forgive us for foolishly sponsoring a bungling stranger. But for you there will be none. Lord Tsekuin and I will take your head with our own swords and lay it before the Hongshu with our own hands. So follow my lead, and do not follow drink, argument, or women."

"Why should I be such a fool, Yezjaro?" said Blade coolly. "Have I shown any signs of being such?"

"You have certainly shown signs of being a man of strong appetites and strong will," said Yezjaro. He turned and strode away. Blade wondered if the instructor had been firing a shot in the dark, or knew something about Blade and Lady Oyasa. It was impossible to say—or ask. Therefore—why worry?

But if Yezjaro did know something . . . Blade decided to start keeping his mouth as tightly shut with Yezjaro as with all the other *dabuni.*

The day for the departure on the Journey of Obedience dawned gray and damp. But the sun broke through the clouds as the party began assembling in the outer courtyard of the castle. It took nearly an hour to assemble the hundred and fifty-odd people, from Lord Tsekuin down to the youngest baggage boy, with all the animals, litters, and wagons. By the time everyone was lined up, the sky overhead was blue, and a brisk wind was drying off the ground and the leaves of the trees. It was weather for a more cheerful occasion.

As it was, not even the priestess of Kunkoi sounded convinced when she declared the clearing of the sky to be a good omen for Lord Tsekuin's safe return. She sounded to Blade like someone trying to convince herself of this so that her voice wouldn't shake too much as she intoned the ritual blessings. She certainly didn't convince anyone else. Yezjaro and Doifuzan managed at least not to look openly gloomy, but not all the *dabuni* were as self-controlled. Most of the servants looked like men sentenced to death, and the women were openly weeping.

Lady Oyasa once more threw etiquette to the winds and came out in a litter to watch the party depart. She did not risk saying anything to Blade. Instead she contented herself with kissing her departing Lord's gloved hand, in the formal manner of a heroine from one of the epic poems. Then she climbed back into her litter. But she left the curtains open, and Blade saw her eyes swing toward him and linger briefly as he spurred his horse toward the outer gate.

The party kept up a good pace until they had reached the bottom of the castle's hill and were well out on the plains. The men on foot had to practically jog to keep up, but no one fell out, complained, or even seemed tired. It was as though they were all eager to get out of the castle and well on their way toward Deyun.

Certainly Blade felt better for being out of the castle and on the way to the Hongshu's capital. Sun, fresh air, a good horse under him, a journey to someplace new—for the moment that was enough to keep him happy.

But then this was not his home, and he had some hope of avoiding the fate of Lord Tsekuin and his clan, no matter what that might be. This set him apart from the others, and always would.

Blade was reminded of just how far apart he and the others were when they reached the Simu River. On the far side of that river was a small hill. The top of the hill was the last place where a man could look back and see the castle.

Each man did look back as he reached the top. Each man had the same expression on his face—even Yezjaro. It was the expression of a man looking back on a place he never expected to see again.

12

The eight-day journey to Deyun was almost a vacation. The weather was good, the roads were straight, level, dry, and easy to ride on, the accommodations along the way surprisingly comfortable. The scenery mixed green fields of young grain, villages with pale yellow thatched roofs, and long stretches of dark forest.

Nothing whatever happened during those eight days. The miles vanished one by one under the hooves of the horses and the sandals of the men on foot. On the seventh day they came in sight of the sea. In the afternoon they moved north along the coast road, passing carts and porters carrying seaweed, a dozen kinds of dried fish, and gear for the ships and boats whose red and brown sails dotted the sea. The crash of the waves on gravel beaches and the smell of salt water were around them. They camped that night in a thick grove of trees that looked like birches but smelled to Blade more like pines. Blade and Yezjaro sat around a campfire long after everyone except the assigned guards had gone to sleep, drinking quietly and thinking out loud about what tomorrow might bring.

"If it brings anything," said Yezjaro. "I suspect the Hongshu and his chancellors will do nothing small against us. They will wait until we thrust our own heads upon the block before they bring the sword down. Meanwhile they will take considerable pleasure in watching us walk with our hands at our sword hilts, waiting for the enemy to strike, fearing that each moment will be our last."

"Perhaps," said Blade.

"You hope that perhaps we have been concerned to no purpose?"

"Yes."

Yezjaro laughed. "So do I, and without shame. I too hope to die in my bed with my concubines and servants lamenting my passing, if it can be done without dishonor. But I think we are hoping for what cannot be. We will be welcomed with open arms—but they will be open only to strike us down."

The "open arms" were very much on display when they rode into Deyun the next morning.

Two magnificently armored horsemen with the badge of the Hongshu on their shields met the party at the edge of the city. They led the way through Deyun's miles of winding streets, uphill, downhill, across large canals and small rivers. The route took them past every sort of shop and booth imaginable, past garbage dumps that made Blade wrinkle up his nose in disgust, past parks with every blade of grass and leaf practically manicured into a perfect pattern. Blade guessed that Deyun might easily hold more than a million people.

At the base of a hill they passed one entire quarter that was enclosed by a high stone wall painted glossy yellow. An entrance was marked by a gate twenty feet high, flanked on either side by masses of carved wooden reliefs extending for a hundred feet. Blade was about to ask Yezjaro what this quarter was, when he got a better look at the reliefs. After that, he didn't need to ask.

The reliefs were the most magnificent erotic sculpture Blade had ever seen. They were not stylized either, unlike much of the art Blade had seen in Gaikon. They were totally explicit and remarkably comprehensive. Blade made a mental resolution to come back to the gates some time before he left Deyun and get a better look at the reliefs—if only to see if they left out anything that a man and a woman could possibly do with each other.

He very much wished he had a good camera and a few rolls of color film.

Yezjaro noticed where Blade's attention was wandering, and grinned. "Ah yes, the warm gates. They are famous throughout Gaikon. A city within a city, it is said, whose ladies are so powerful that they may pass through tunnels barred to all others to do their work even within the Hongshu's palace itself! But remember what I said about your strong appetites and what you must do about them."

"Oh, I will remember, Yezjaro," said Blade. "You do the same. Nothing I have seen or heard of you suggests that you are a *weak* man in such matters."

Eventually they reached the wall around the Hongshu's palace. It made the wall of the warm gates quarter look like a barrier of toothpicks and sugar cubes. It rose forty feet high and was twenty feet thick, crowned with towers rising another thirty feet. From every slit in the railings and every window and balcony of the towers armed men peered out and down. The gates were thirty feet high and contained enough iron and timber to build a fair-sized ship. Nothing short of starvation—or home dimension heavy artillery—could bring down the Hongshu's fortress.

"The official name for this area is the *Jeshun Doi*," said Yezjaro.

"That means—?" said Blade.

"The House of the Mighty Warlike Power," replied Yezjaro.

"The Hongshus don't mince words, do they?"

"Not unless it serves their purpose. Which it—wait, here comes our welcoming committee." Blade heard the sound of trumpets from within the gates, then the gates themselves began to open with a rumble and a squeal.

Just inside the palace wall was a level field, completely surrounded by more walls, towers, and the roofs of houses, but offering room enough to fight a good-sized battle. For a moment Blade thought they were going to have to do just that. A cordon of armed men—spearmen, archers, and *dabuni* with drawn swords—stretched across the field in front of them. Then he noticed a tall, thin, elderly man on a ridiculously small horse riding out toward them.

"Lord Geron, the Hongshu's second chancellor," whispered Yezjaro. "In theory it does us great honor, sending him out to greet us. But it is no secret that Geron's head is more full of schemes and plots than all the other five chancellors put together. They call him the Hongshu's pet wolf."

The pet wolf exchanged bows and all the appropriate phrases with Lord Tsekuin. Then he signaled to his guards. They ran forward, herding the servants of the party away from their horses and baggage toward the gate. Behind the guards came a horde of palace servants, as silent and efficient as well-oiled machinery, scooping up the fallen baggage and leading off the pack animals. When they were gone, Lord Geron turned his horse and led Lord Tsekuin's party toward the inner gate.

Beyond that gate were the main stables, where they dismounted and emptied their saddlebags. Then Lord Geron and a dozen tough-looking *dabuni* led the way into the heart of the palace. The paths, corridors, and alleys within it seemed laid out to no plan or purpose.

"Except that of confusing anybody who doesn't know his way around?" Blade asked Yezjaro.

"Precisely," said the instructor. "It is a maze that will drive any stranger without a guide mad. Assuming he lives that long, between the guards and the traps."

"The servants must know their way around."

"They do. But they are also sworn never to leave the palace and to die before revealing any of its secrets. Those who try to escape die by torture. No, the Hongshu's servants usually live and die within these walls. Many of them are the children of other servants, so they truly know nothing but this maze from birth to death."

Blade nodded. The Hongshu was obviously grimly determined to be as unassailable as possible. There would be no easy way of striking at him here, at the heart of his power. Unless those tunnels from the warm gates quarter could be made passages for something less welcome than courtesans? Perhaps, but it was not something to worry about now.

The palace covered as much ground as a fair-sized city, but their wanderings nonetheless eventually came to an end. More silent attendants led the various *dabuni* of the party to the tiny cubicles reserved for them. Blade sat down on the mats that covered the floor with a sigh of relief. He was not particularly tired. But it was good to be out of that gloomy, bristling maze, and in a place with solid walls around him.

On the morning of the seventeenth day in the palace, Blade was sitting in the same spot, in the same cubicle. Only the mats were different. They were changed every three days by those silent, swift-footed palace servants. For all that had happened otherwise, Blade might as well have spent the entire seventeen days sitting on the floor of his cubicle.

It hadn't taken Blade more than a few of those days to realize what tactic the Hongshu had adopted for attacking Lord Tsekuin. He would have Lord Tsekuin and his men wait—and wait, and wait, and wait until somebody's patience snapped. Hopefully it would be Lord Tsekuin's patience, since that would give the Hongshu the best excuse for the deadliest action.

For eight days Lord Tsekuin had gone out with Yezjaro and Doifuzan, hoping to set a time for his audience with the Hongshu. For eight days he came back, after hearing that no time could be set until he had been approved in the etiquette of the court.

So for the *next* eight days Lord Tsekuin and the other two had gone out, seeking someone who might test and pass him in court etiquette. That turned out to be the search for the little man who wasn't there. Each time, Lord Tsekuin had returned with his face more and more flushed with barely suppressed rage.

One of these mornings he wasn't going to be able to suppress that rage. Even if by some miracle Lord Tsekuin didn't fly into a rage, Blade daily expected one of the *dabuni* to blow up. Fortunately, that hadn't happened either. In fact, so little had happened that Blade was beginning to wonder if he wouldn't have seen more of Gaikon by staying in the castle.

He stretched and stood up. He was doing his daily exercises when Yezjaro came in. The instructor was walking more briskly than usual, and his face was pale.

"Blade, Lord Tsekuin has gone out to seek a meeting with Lord Geron. He has gone by himself. Neither Doifuzan nor I nor any of the other *dabuni* is with him. And he has taken both his swords."

That was bad news anyway you looked at it. There was no need to go armed in the palace. If the Hongshu was determined that you wouldn't leave the palace alive, that was that. A sword would do no good. In fact, to even draw a sword in the palace was a mortal offense to the Hongshu, an offense for which he could impose any penalties he saw fit. Blade did not turn pale himself, but he understood why Yezjaro had done so.

Together they went out into the common room into which all the cubicles led. They sat down on the mats and joined a dozen other early rising *dabuni* at a breakfast of porridge and boiled fish. Blade noticed that both Yezjaro and Doifuzan left their breakfasts practically untouched.

The rest of the *dabuni* trickled out and ate breakfast. Many of them ate greedily, their appetites unaffected by the tension. But the palace servants never paused in refilling the bowls and plates. Blade tried to calculate how much this charade might be costing the Hongshu. Then he shrugged. It made no difference. If the Hongshu's plot succeeded, he would have control of the diamond mines. If he had control of the diamond mines, they would give him wealth enough to feed ten thousand men for ten thousand years.

The morning plodded wearily on. One hour since Lord Tsekuin had gone out. Two hours. Three. It was getting on toward lunchtime, and Doifuzan and Yezjaro were getting on toward nervous breakdowns. They were both pacing up and down like caged animals. Their faces were the same dirty white as the breakfast porridge.

Finally Yezjaro couldn't stand it any longer. He tightened his sash and pulled on his sandals. "I am going to see Lord Geron and try to find our own lord. Doifuzan, will you join me?"

The older *dabuno* hesitated for a moment, then nodded. "I will."

"Good." Both warriors strode out, wearing their

swords and grim expressions. They made no move to invite anybody else to join them, Blade included. Behind them remained a tension that had suddenly frozen into something that could be almost cut in slices. No one moved or spoke, and for a while Blade would have sworn that nobody breathed.

The minutes dragged on. They had added up to another half hour before anyone felt like speaking. Even then it was only casual words in low voices.

Blade was just turning to a man sitting beside him when the sound of a gong came booming down the corridor outside. Several more joined in, making an echoing, painful din.

Faintly over the roar Blade heard angry shouts. Then, unmistakably, he heard running feet approaching along the corridor. Blade sprang to his feet, but remembered just in time not to draw his sword. The running feet approached the door to the room and stopped. The door flew open with a grinding crash.

One of the palace servants stood there, showing the first emotion Blade had ever seen in one of those silent men. Sweat was pouring off his face and his hands were shaking as he stepped forward.

"Horrible! Horrible! Nothing like it was ever seen! Nothing!"

"What is it, you fool?" snapped Blade. "What's happened?"

"Lord Tsekuin—your Lord Tsekuin—quarreled with Lord Geron. Lord Tsekuin—*he drew his sword*. He drew his sword against Lord Geron and wounded him. Perhaps killed him. I don't know. I couldn't watch. I ran. Oh, Kunkoi have mercy on us!"

13

By the time the servant had finished, everyone in the room was on his feet, staring at the man. The *dabuni* began to curse and growl with rage.

"Treachery!"

"That slimy son of six Warm Gates whores has—!"

"Our lord is doomed. We must—!"

"Kunkoi be my witness, I'll—!"

Nobody would let anybody else finish a sentence. Half the men couldn't even talk coherently. The *dabuni* began to stalk about, raising their hands and swearing blood-curdling oaths. The palace servant watched from the door, frozen and wide-eyed with amazement and growing fear.

From a corner of the room, Blade also watched his fellow *dabuni* working themselves up into a rage. He knew this uproar among Lord Tsekuin's men could explode at any second into a bloody shambles. He seemed to be the only man in the room who was keeping his head. If one of those idiots drew his sword . . .

One of the younger *dabuni* headed toward the door. Blade stepped out of his corner to intercept the man. The warrior's hand flew to his sword. Blade smashed a foot like a battering ram into the *dabuno's* stomach. The man flew backward, hitting the wall with a sickening thud, and collapsed. Blade sprang backward until he stood between the open door and thirty-odd furious *dabuni.*

Another man came at Blade, his sword already half-drawn as he came within Blade's striking range. No doubt he saw that Blade had not drawn his sword yet, but he expected he would soon. The stranger *dabuno* would be an easy victim. Then on to avenge his shamed lord!

That was a mistake. Blade came in low, one hand driving up under the attacker's sword arm, the other up under his chin. The man's sword flew out of its scabbard and soared high into the air. It struck the ceiling with a clang, bounced off, and nearly skewered the gaping palace servant as it came down. He fell over backward in his frantic haste to get clear, scrambled to his feet, and dashed away down the corridor as though hungry tigers were at his heels.

The *dabuno* also flew into the air. As he came down, Blade's whirling leg scythed into him. He flew across the room, hit the floor on his belly, and slid into one of the cubicles with his chin scraping the mats.

For a long moment everyone in the room seemed paralyzed by Blade's explosion of action. Deadly skill in unarmed combat was well known in Gaikon—the *jinais* were notoriously expert at it. But for a *dabuno* to have such skill—well, it suggested that he had the soul of a skulker by night or an assassin, rather than that of a warrior who fought in bright day with bright steel. So Blade had kept the skill of his hands and feet a secret.

Blade took advantage of his opponents' brief paralysis to unknot his sash. His two swords dropped to the mats. He kicked them aside and dropped back into karate stance. Now that he had disarmed himself, none of the other *dabuni* could come at him with a sword without disgracing themselves. Of course, if some of them were maddened beyond the point of worrying about honor, and did draw—well, Blade had no illusions that he could survive bare-handed against a swordsman of Gaikon who knew what to do and what to expect.

Once again silence and tension in the room grew thick enough to slice like bread. The only noise was the faint whisper of quick, shallow breathing, the only movement the blinking of eyes. Blade felt that all those eyes were focused on him, trying to guess what he might do next. He found that he wasn't quite sure himself. As long as none of the *dabuni* were ready to be singled out, Blade suspected he could hold. But if they came in a rush, four or five of them . . .

Then the tension dissolved as Yezjaro and Doifuzan burst through the door behind Blade. They dashed into the center of the room and the other *dabuni* hastily made a clear space for them.

Both men were pale and held themselves unnaturally straight as they stood in the middle of the room, hands behind their backs. But their eyes moved steadily around the room, taking in everything. Their expressions hardened. Doifuzan managed to keep his face almost under control. But Yezjaro's face set in a savage glare that made the *dabuni* unable to meet his eyes. It seemed that anyone he looked at directly would go up in a cloud of greasy smoke and leave nothing behind but a charred spot on the mats.

Yezjaro was also the first to speak. "What is this—this stupid running around like a bunch of chickens? Have you all gone mad? We've enough trouble already without you fools adding to it!" He glared around the room, daring anyone to move or speak.

There were men twice Yezjaro's age among the *dabuni* in the room, men Blade had heard mutter about "loud-mouthed young swordsmen who didn't know enough to properly respect their elders." For a moment Blade wasn't sure that Yezjaro's outburst hadn't made things worse instead of better. He crouched, ready to move forward to pull down anyone who might draw against Yezjaro.

Fortunately Doifuzan agreed with this hot-headed younger comrade. "The Honorable Instructor has asked a very good question, brothers. What folly has driven you to this rage? It cannot serve your lord, it cannot serve yourselves or your honor. What purpose does it serve, then? I ask. Shall I be answered?" Doifuzan's voice was low, but every word dropped clearly and precisely into the silence. The first *dabuno* was normally a quiet man, whose words were few and formal. But he was respected as much for his personal qualities as for his position. When he did speak, the *dabuni* of Lord Tsekuin listened.

One of the *dabuni* took on himself the unwelcome task of answering, "Honorable Instructor, Honorable First *Dabuno*, it was thus. The news of our lord's shame—"

He told the whole story in a few sentences. When he had finished, he fell on his knees on the mat before Doifuzan. After a moment, the other *dabuni* did the same. Only Blade was left in his combat stance by the door.

Doifuzan pulled at his chin. "You tell a story that is not to the credit of your wits. You tell it plainly, which is honorable. For that I praise you. But by the splendor of Kunkoi, I will not praise the folly that so nearly led you into—*monstrous* action, that would have doomed us all! Only the courage and swiftness of your brother Blade stood between all of you and the price of your own folly. The brother Blade, a man I have heard many of you speak of with scorn. Speak of him thus no more, however long you may yet have tongues to speak with. Instead, bow to him, for this day he has done much for the honor of the clan—and may yet do more."

The last words snapped out with an angry edge to them. For a moment the *dabuni* once more seemed paralyzed. Then slowly, one by one, they turned and bowed deeply to Blade.

As he returned the bows, Blade found it hard to keep his face straight. Suddenly he was a man to be honored among Lord Tsekuin's warriors. But just as suddenly, Lord Tsekuin's own folly had made him a lord who would soon have no need for warriors at all.

The Hongshu's axe did not fall on Lord Tsekuin at once.

Yezjaro told Blade what the normal course of events was in such a breach of etiquette.

"Lord Tsekuin will of course have to commit ritual suicide. Of course he will also have the right to make a final request of the Hongshu, who must grant it. That is ancient custom. But after that Lord Tsekuin must die by his own hand. His household will be abolished, the clan stricken from the records and laws of Gaikon, and all the people scattered. The castle and all its lands will be confiscated by the Hongshu."

"Including the diamond mines?"

"Especially the diamond mines," said Yezjaro bitterly. "The Hongshu's dream has been realized."

"What happens to the *dabuni* after they are scattered?"

"They become *uroi–dabuni* without masters. Their fates are as their own skill and wisdom and the will of Kunkoi would have it. No act that even the Hongshu can call rebellion has taken place, thanks largely to your quick wits. Therefore I suppose in time most of those who once served Lord Tsekuin will find other masters elsewhere in Gaikon, and come to whatever destiny may be theirs in as much peace as ever falls to the lot of a *dabuno*."

Those were the instructor's words. But Blade's trained ears heard other meanings lurking beneath those words. Here in the palace the walls had ears. It would be foolish to even ask what Yezjaro had in mind. There would be no answer in any case. But Blade was certain of one thing. The Hongshu and his servant Lord Geron had not heard the last of Lord Tsekuin's *dabuni*.

To change the subject, Blade asked, "Has Lord Tsekuin decided what his last request shall be?"

"Not yet," said Yezjaro. "I think he wishes to give it some thought, to make it as memorable as possible. In his position, would you not do likewise?"

It was several more days before Lord Tsekuin reached his decision. It was several days after that before he announced it. Meanwhile the *dabuni* stayed silently in their cubicles, except for those allowed to leave the palace to take the bad news back to the castle. Those who remained ate little and said less. The knowledge that their lord was disgraced and they themselves doomed to be cast adrift seemed to be sinking in.

Blade detected a certain resentment against him growing again during those days. Perhaps he had indeed saved them from making fatal mistakes in their anger. But he was still a stranger, a man with no roots in Gaikon, a man who could easily pick up his spear and vanish over the horizon if necessary. Blade was particularly careful during those days to keep his mouth shut and hide his comparative detachment from Lord Tsekuin's fate.

Nearly two weeks after the fatal incident, Lord Tsekuin finally announced his decision. Yezjaro,

Doifuzan, and Blade were the only ones present when he announced it.

"I shall play a master game of *Hu* against the Hongshu," he said, twining his fingers together. He had lost enough weight so that his hands seemed as thin and pale as those of a skeleton.

Blade's first thought was, "Is that all?" Then he looked at Yezjaro and Doifuzan. They were waiting expectantly for more.

"Yes," said Lord Tsekuin. "I shall play a master game with the Hongshu. And you"—he shot a finger out at Blade—"shall take your spear and be the first warrior of my hand."

That made no sense to Blade. But obviously it meant a good deal to the other two warriors. Both had grim smiles on their faces—the first smiles Blade had seen there for weeks.

"Ah, Blade," said Doifuzan. "I see you do not understand what our lord would have you do?"

Blade bowed and spoke formally. "Honorable First *Dabuno*, I confess my ignorance and ask that you enlighten me."

"It is simple. The master game of *Hu* is played by the Hongshu with each of the five pieces of the hand represented by a living *dabuno*. You will be the first warrior, the most powerful piece of the hand. It is known that with your spear you are all but invincible, so this is proper."

Doifuzan's smile broadened. "You will honorably represent our lord, Blade. And you will make this game of *Hu* memorable for the Hongshu as well. When a piece captures another in it, they fight. To the death."

Blade bowed. "I am honored by our lord's confidence in me." There was nothing else he could appropriately say. Besides, this was certainly being at the center of things!

14

Blade stood in the first warrior's black square and stared out across the enormous *Hu*-board pattern that covered the entire floor of the huge chamber. The black and white squares gleamed in the light of the lamps swinging from the beams overhead. Behind him Lord Tsekuin sat on a chair cushioned with white silk. At the opposite corner of the board sat the Hongshu. Beside him Lord Geron lay on a litter. Lord Tsekuin had not wounded the second chancellor as seriously as it had been believed at first. But it would be several weeks more before he could walk about normally. The side of his face that was now swathed in bandages would be scarred for life.

Beside Lord Tsekuin sat Doifuzan. Other than the two players and their companions, the only people in the chamber were the five "pieces" of each player's hand. Blade had wondered why the Hongshu thought he would be safe facing a man whom he had disgraced and doomed.

"You may wonder that," Doifuzan had said. "But not aloud. To even think of striking at the person of the Hongshu is an abomination. Were any of us to do that, the whole clan would be swept from the land. Castles and huts alike would burn, fields would be plowed up and sown with salt, men, women, children, warriors, and peasants—all would perish by fire or steel or slow torture. Do not speak the least word of rebellion against the person of the Hongshu."

Blade saw the wisdom of that. It was not the time or place to point out that dead Hongshus execute no rebels. It was also not the time to ask what might be done against other enemies than the Hongshu himself. Blade was sure that Yezjaro and Doifuzan were already thinking about this. He was just as sure they would not welcome his questions about it.

Blade threw a brief glance at the Hongshu. He was on the small side, but he wore his hair tied higher than usual and sat very erect to conceal the fact. He looked lean and in fighting trim, although a full beard suggested something about his face that he preferred to conceal. His eyes moved continuously about the chamber. In another man this might have given the impression of restlessness. In this man it gave the impression of a ceaseless curiosity, a constant ferreting out of other people's secrets.

A formidable man, Blade suspected. Perhaps there was reason why even the Hongshu's enemies preferred his iron-handed rule to that of the present overeducated, weak-willed emperor.

But the politics of Gaikon meant nothing one way or the other in this chamber. Blade turned his eyes to the five *dabuni* of the Hongshu's hand. The man had certainly picked them for size. There wasn't one of them less than six feet tall or lighter than two hundred pounds. Their swords and spears were in proportion. But did they have skill to match their brawn?

All four of Blade's own comrades were at least competent fighters. Two carried spears, two carried swords. But Blade suspected he was going to wind up doing most of the fighting.

The sound of another of Gaikon's thousands of gongs broke into his thoughts. The Hongshu rose from his chair and stepped forward to stand beside his first warrior. Lord Tsekuin did the same with Blade. Lord Tsekuin bowed deeply; the Hongshu bowed much less deeply. The Hongshu stepped back and intoned in a surprisingly deep voice:

"We meet here in the master game of *Hu*. Such is the wish of Lord Tsekuin. Such wish is his right by the laws and customs of proper obedience, as established by the Hongshu Korlo in the fifty-fourth year of the power of this house. Let it be witnessed that this is his wish, and to it we consent."

Lord Geron and Doifuzan spoke together. "It is witnessed."

The Hongshu nodded slowly. "Then let the game commence." He sat down again, while the gongs sounded again from above. Then he folded his arms and leaned back in his chair, waiting for Lord Tsekuin to declare the first move.

Even with only ten pieces on its forty-eight-square board, *Hu* was a complicated game. Each of the five pieces of each hand—first warrior, first and second swordsman, first and second spearman—had about thirty different moves. Some they could make at all times, others only under certain conditions. Blade remembered his remark when Yezjaro first summarized the rules and moves for him.

"It sounds like a long game."

"It is. Two truly skilled players have been known to sit at a board for three days continuously, without food or sleep. A normal game can last six or seven hours."

But this game would not last even a few hours, let alone several days. There would be no captures, only death, and the blood on the tiled squares would be entirely real.

The gongs died away. From behind him Blade heard the rustle of Lord Tsekuin's robes as he sat down. Then the man's voice rang out in the sudden silence of the chamber, loud enough to echo.

"Second spearman—*Jufon* move to square six-five."

Both players devoted their first few moves to maneuvering their five pieces out toward the center of the board. The Hongshu seemed to prefer a more open formation, Lord Tsekuin a tight one. Blade suspected that was to make it easier for him to move into action against any of his five possible opponents. There were strategies in the regular game of *Hu* built around the first warrior in just that way. They made even more sense here.

After that came a quick series of another half-dozen moves, most of them unnecessarily intricate. When that was finished, the two clusters of warriors were almost exactly where they had started. Blade suspected the two players were trying to either impress or confuse each other with their skill at the more intricate moves of the game.

But both players were too experienced to let a show-off opponent's tricks bother them. When the sequence of moves was done, Blade shot a quick look behind him. Lord Tsekuin sat motionless in his chair, arms crossed on his chest, his face a mask as immobile as if it had been cast in bronze. Blade's respect for the doomed lord rose. Keeping that iron calm under the circumstances was admirable.

A long silent pause followed. The moment for the first blood was approaching. Blade knew that neither player was hesitating out of any fear of that moment. But now the price of a wrong move had suddenly risen. Now it could throw away a warrior of the hand, and perhaps the game.

It was the Hongshu's turn now. One of his swordsmen made a simple move out to the right. Simple—but it brought him to where one of Lord Tsekuin's spearmen could engage him by any of half a dozen moves.

The Hongshu had thrown out his challenge. Now the decision lay in Lord Tsekuin's hands. Blood now or later?

Lord Tsekuin rose to the challenge. He called out a move in clipped, cool tones. The spearman moved to engage. He was the youngest of the five *dabuni* in Tsekuin's hand. Could he have any chance against the Hongshu's swordsman?

His opponent was half again as large as the spearman and looked larger still. With a rasp of metal he drew his sword. The spearman's weapon rose into position and he dropped into fighting stance. The silence in the chamber deepened. The two opponents stood motionless, their weapons raised. From where Blade stood, he couldn't even see them breathe.

Suddenly the two frozen figures in the center of the chamber exploded in sound and movement. The swordsman's weapon swung wide, leaving him open to the spearman's thrust. The spearpoint flashed forward. The sword whipped back as fast as it had swung out. Steel point and steel blade crashed against each other with an echoing clang that filled the chamber. The spearpoint dropped down, the sword blade rose up. It flicked out toward the young spearman, but he seemed to twist aside at the last second. He stood as his opponent pulled his sword back and raised it again. Blade wondered why the young man didn't turn back to face his opponent.

Then the spearman's point dropped further, to rest against the floor. His fingers opened and the spear clattered to the floor. A moment later the spearman followed it. As he struck the floor and lay full length on it, blood began to gush from the wound in his side, under his armpit. Blade looked more closely. The gash went in halfway through the chest. Had it gone straight into the heart, with that single split second blow?

As if to answer Blade's question, the spearman gave a final convulsive jerk, gurgled, coughed, and lay still. Blood trickled out of his mouth to join the spreading pool on the tiles.

Blade took a tighter grip on his own spear. That was a quick kill even by Gaikon's deadly standards. It now seemed quite likely that the Hongshu's *dabuni* were as skilled as they were big.

The Hongshu wore a smug, arrogant grin. Blade risked another look behind him, at Lord Tsekuin and Doifuzan. Then he looked again. Both men had their eyes fixed on the Hongshu. As his grin broadened, they began to have trouble keeping their own faces straight. Blade swung his eyes back across the body on the floor to the triumphant Hongshu. Then the light dawned for him.

Lord Tsekuin had deliberately sacrificed the young spearman, who was after all the least important *dabuno* of his hand. He had cold-bloodedly sacrificed him to make the Hongshu overconfident. Judging by the other man's expression, he had succeeded. And the young spearman had gone to his death with no regard for anything but his lord's orders, although he knew what was coming.

Blade suspected that there were two games being played today. There was the deadly master game of *Hu* here in the chamber. There was another, larger, deadlier game being played for far higher stakes all over Gaikon, of which this game of *Hu* might be only a part.

Blade clutched his spear so tightly in both hands that his knuckles stood out white. He managed to give a slight tremble to both his lower lip and his knees, and swallowed rapidly several times. He wanted to give the impression of a man suddenly realizing the deadly stakes of this game, and half-unnerved by his discovery. As he turned away from the two men behind him his eyes briefly met Doifuzan's. The old *dabuno's* lips flickered apart in a brief smile, one that the Hongshu would never see. Blade turned back to stare across the chamber at the enemy. The Hongshu was rubbing his hands on the knees of his white silk trousers, and the visible half of Lord Geron's face was split by a broad grin.

Good. They looked like men who would be half-blind with triumph and anticipation of an easy victory. Blade relaxed his grip on his spear and waited for Lord Tsekuin to announce his next move. He suspected it would bring him into the play.

He was wrong. Lord Tsekuin apparently decided it would help if he also acted like a man who had lost his self-control because of the death of the spearman. He indulged in a flurry of moves, simple and complex, varying them without any apparent pattern. He didn't pay much attention to the Hongshu's responses, either. Blade hoped Lord Tsekuin wouldn't carry the act *too* far. If the Hongshu decided to move in for a quick victory while Tsekuin was doing his imitation of a frightened, indecisive man, things could get very nasty very quickly.

The Hongshu didn't. But then he was obviously one of those men who savored watching his enemy sweat in fear before striking. Here he couldn't wait two weeks before striking, as he had done before. But he could wait a few minutes, and then a few minutes more—and then a few minutes beyond that.

The minutes added up until nearly an hour had passed since the spearman's death. The aimless maneuvering went on, neither side pushing their warriors into a fight. Blade threw occasional looks behind him. Had Lord Tsekuin *really* lost his head and his skill? He began to wonder. But each time he looked, Doifuzan met his eyes with a faint smile or nod.

The maneuvering went on for a few minutes more. But now it had a purpose. One move at a time, Lord Tsekuin was shifting Blade. Soon he would be within a single move of battle with any of the Hongshu's five *dabuni*.

The ruler of Gaikon was too filled with anticipation of his easy victory to notice what was happening. Blade made his last necessary move. The Hongshu shifted a spearman in a minor move that still left him within range of Blade. Blade deliberately dropped his spear to keep up the act of being nervous and panicky.

Then behind him Blade heard Lord Tsekuin's voice.

"*Sha* move to square four-seven." Three quick steps and Blade was facing the Hongshu's second swordsman. To Blade it seemed the room had suddenly become even quieter than before.

In a regular bout, Blade would have started a slow circle around his opponent, forcing him to shift position, testing his footwork, perhaps trying to disorient him. But here the fighters had to stay within their squares. All they could do was freeze into their stances and hold position, weapons aloft and ready, eyes watching for the slightest sign of an attack.

Blade was determined to wait and give his opponent the first blow. It was a gamble, since he couldn't leave the square to avoid his enemy's sword. But it was only a small gamble. Blade knew how fast he was. The other man didn't.

A slight flickering of the swordsman's arm muscles was all the warning Blade had. The sword leaped high, ready to slash down at Blade's skull. Then it leaped sideways and came whistling at Blade's side—or where Blade's side should have been. But Blade recognized the stroke—a clumsy version of Yezjaro's own "flying bird cut." The defense against it was something built into his reflexes by long hours of practice against the instructor.

Blade sprang back on legs like steel springs. The tip of the sword whistled by, inches from his stomach. The sword swung wide. Blade leaped in again, holding the spear out to his right in a vertical guard. The return cut with the sword crashed into the spear shaft. Again the clash of metal echoed through the chamber. As the sword leaped up again, Blade drove the spear downward. The sharp edge of the spearhead slashed down the second swordsman's left leg from knee to ankle. Flesh gaped open and blood sluiced down on to the floor.

The second swordsman let out a howl of surprise and pain and stared wide-eyed at Blade. He seemed bothered more by his opponent's unexpected skill than by his own wound. But he hadn't lost any courage. His sword whistled down again three times in rapid succession—left, right, right. But his aim was poor and his footwork slowed by the wound. Blade considered using the prongs on the spear to disarm the man the way he had disarmed Captain Jawai. But why bother? There was no need to put on a show here—just a well-done kill.

The sword rose again and seemed to hover edge-on in front of Blade. He raised the spear, holding it horizontally in front of him. The swordsman launched a cut at Blade's ribs. Blade sprang back, shifting to a one-handed grip on the spear. The massive muscles of his right arm snapped the spear horizontally forward, straight into the swordsman's throat. Flesh, blood vessels, windpipe parted as neatly as if Blade had swung a giant razor. Blade jerked the spear back. The swordsman stood for a moment, blood fountaining from his gaping neck, the life going out of his eyes. Then he fell, landing with a *splat* in the spreading pool of his own blood.

Blade pulled off his tunic, which had been spattered by the spraying blood of his opponent's death-wound. He wiped his bloody spearhead with it. Then he spread the tunic over the dead man's head, stepped back into the middle of his own square, and pounded his spearbutt three times on the floor.

It was the signal of victory. It was also the signal for a sudden flurry of murmuring and whispering. Blade was conscious that every eye in the room was fixed on him. Then the four survivors of the Hongshu's hand started looking at each other. Uncertainty was in their eyes.

Their master's voice slashed through the silence. "Why stand and gape, you fools? He who lies there did nothing worthy of a wise *dabuno*. He doomed himself by forgetting who had instructed his opponent. That was no true victory we saw. That was a fool's bungling suicide!"

The Hongshu's voice was loud and harsh. But Blade realized that he was trying to reassure himself more than his four *dabuni*. He was certainly not improving their spirits. Blade noticed sour looks on their faces, sour looks directed at their master.

Before the sour looks could turn into open rebellion, the Hongshu called out his move. Blade watched. Would he now send his first warrior or first swordsman forward against Blade?

Instead the first swordsman moved back and around, on to the flank of the first warrior. Blade was still within easy reach of both spearmen. Would Lord Tsekuin—?

Lord Tsekuin would. Blade found himself face-to-face with the opposing first spearman. He considered his next move.

The first two kills had been crude, at least by Gaikon's highest standards. How to make more of an impression with the next one? An impression not only on the Hongshu's mind, but also on the other three opposing *dabuni*?

Then Blade grinned. There was a standard technique in Gaikon spear-fighting. In the hands of the average *dabuno*, it was more spectacular than deadly. But Blade was not the average *dabuno*. His arms were stronger and his eyes and reflexes faster. He could make the "spectacle" turn deadly.

Blade stepped back, out of range of a quick thrust from his opponent. He raised the spear over his head, holding it horizontally in both hands. Then he began to whirl it, his hands shifting with steadily increasing speed. The spearman's eyes drifted up to the whirling spear. No doubt he knew perfectly well that such a whirling spear could not be stopped and thrust forward without giving more than enough warning to an opponent. So did the Hongshu. He could not keep a sneer off his face as he watched Blade's spear whirl and listened to the mounting hiss as it cut the air. If one of Lord Tsekuin's men was going to make a fool of himself this way, so much the better.

Once he had settled into a steady rhythm, Blade could keep a spear going like this for half an hour without thinking about it at all. He kept his eyes and mind focused on the spearman, with occasional glances at the Hongshu. He wanted to go on long enough to get everyone thinking he must be getting tired. Not long enough to really get tired, though. His one-shot kill might not come off. Years of single-combat experience told him to keep plenty of strength in reserve.

He whirled the spear faster. Now the hiss deepened into a drone, like a distant swarm of bees. He did not bother looking up. He knew that by this time the spear must be only a half-invisible blur above him, like a hummingbird's wings. Sweat began to trickle down his face and chest, and he felt the first twinges of strain in his arm and wrist muscles. It wouldn't be long now.

Definitely it wouldn't be long now. The spearman was beginning to look speculatively at him and to shift his grip on his own weapon. Had he decided Blade was a madman, easily vulnerable? Time to change his mind, then.

Blade focused his attention on the spear for a moment. One, two, three, four more times around. Then his breath exploded out of him in a scream.

"Kiiiiy-a-a-ahhhhh!

The spear froze in midair. Before the spearman could blink an eye, Blade took the one step forward that brought him within thrusting range. The spearman's weapon jerked upward in a futile effort to guard. If the man had tried his own thrust, he might at least have taken Blade with him. As it was, his spear was still rising when Blade's spear drove downward. It drove into the spearman's belly just below the ribs, drove through the spine with a sharp *crack*, and burst out his back in a spray of blood. Blade jerked the spear free and stepped away as the spearman collapsed backward. When the last convulsion subsided, Blade again wiped his spear on the dead man's trousers and turned to face the Hongshu.

This hadn't been quite as spectacular a kill as he might have managed. He had trained himself until he could bring a spear to a stop and pick off a fly on the wall. But why risk missing? The one blow had been struck and the spearman was dead. The Hongshu wasn't particularly happy about it, either. One hand was tightly clutching the arm of his chair, until Blade wondered if the hard black wood would collapse into sawdust under the pressure. He also had the look of a man trying to keep the shock he felt off his face.

Lord Tsekuin and Doifuzan were also fighting to keep their faces expressionless. They looked as though they wanted to throw aside their dignity and applaud or embrace Blade—or both at once.

The three surviving *dabuni* of the Hongshu's hand weren't even trying to look calm. They had seen two of their comrades die under Blade's spear like rats in a dog's jaws. They couldn't avoid wondering who was next. Blade noticed the first warrior looking toward the Hongshu. His face showed a mixture of anticipation and fear. Blade guessed that this time it would be the Hongshu who forced the combat. Probably between the two first warriors.

Blade had guessed right. The Hongshu's first warrior was drawing his sword and raising it into position as he stepped forward. A simple move through four squares, and he stood in the square to Blade's right. Blade raised his spear and turned to face the man.

He was the largest of the Hongshu's outsized warriors, nearly six and a half feet tall. But there was no fat on his massive frame, only supple muscle. His feet moved with a delicacy and assurance that told Blade this man might be faster than he looked. Blade decided not to plan in advance any particular way of dealing with the first warrior. He would try a few exchanges first, to reveal the man's weaknesses, relying on his own speed to keep himself safe.

Blade almost wasn't fast enough. A sudden *whuff*, and the first warrior's sword split the air beside Blade's ear. A few inches closer, and it would have split his head as neatly as a grapefruit. Blade aimed a thrust at the man's thigh. The sword blocked the thrust, then smashed the spear aside with a blow that nearly tore it out of Blade's hands. If it had landed squarely instead of glancing, it would have chopped the spear in two.

This man definitely wasn't going to be as easy a

victim as the first two. In fact, Blade wasn't even sure that the first warrior was going to be the victim at all. This was an opponent who could and would chop him in two if he slipped at all. Hope was written nakedly all over the Hongshu's face, and even the other two *dabuni* of the enemy's hand wore thin smiles.

The deadly dance went on. Blade soon realized that he couldn't tire this man out. He couldn't force him off-balance—the man handled his two hundred and fifty-plus pounds too well. He couldn't get through his guard with any thrust or stroke that wouldn't leave him dangerously vulnerable. Blade began to get the ugly feeling that this bout would go on and on and on, ending only when one man or the other got lucky.

That wasn't so good. Luck could work for either man. Obviously the two players knew that. Both the Hongshu and Lord Tsekuin wore identical expressions of frozen strain.

More exchanges of cuts and thrusts. Blade now had a small cut in one hip, his opponent an equally small one on his shoulder. Blade still couldn't see any pattern in his opponent's responses that would help him break through the man's guard. He was beginning to wonder if there was one.

Another deafening clang sounded as spear shaft met sword. The shock deflected Blade's spear upward, the point driving over the first warrior's head inches above his tightly bound hair. He didn't seem to notice it at all.

Blade licked dry lips and deliberately made his next thrust a high one, aiming over the head again. He almost aimed too high. The sword came through his open guard and nicked his ribs, and blood trickled again. But the first warrior didn't notice the direction of Blade's thrust.

A light dawned for Blade. The Hongshu's first warrior seemed to have trouble coping with attacks coming in above his eye level. Did he have vision trouble? Or was it just that he so seldom had to look up at anything that it didn't occur to him to look up, even in a fight? Blade didn't care. He knew he had a possible opening.

If he was right. If he was wrong—but he couldn't take more time to confirm his guess. Many more high thrusts, and the first warrior might become aware of his own weak point and extend his guard. Then it would be back to the endless dance, waiting for luck to turn for one fighter or the other.

Blade stepped back. He dropped into a crouch that made him look as though he was planning a thrust into the first warrior's groin. Then he leaped straight up, legs uncoiling in a single snap of powerful muscles. He soared upward like an Olympic high jumper, six feet clear of the floor. At the top of his leap his spear lunged out and down.

The first warrior had just started to raise his eyes and sword to follow Blade when Blade's spear drove down at him. It drove down into him almost vertically between the collarbone and the top rib, plunging through until it came out at the small of his back. With Blade's full descending weight behind it, the spear smashed the first warrior backward onto the floor hard enough to crush his skull. Then Blade let go of the spear and came down with both feet on the fallen man's chest and stomach. He heard more grisly noises as the first warrior's ribs and internal organs gave under the impact of Blade's two hundred and ten pounds.

Blade stepped off the body, pulled out his spear, and backed away into the center of his own square. He had never inflicted so many fatal injuries on one opponent in such a short time.

The Hongshu also looked as though he had lost a good deal of blood. His face had turned the same dirty off-white as the chamber walls, and the hand he raised was shaking slightly.

"Honorable Lord Tsekuin," he called out. His voice was shaking slightly also. "Do you consent that I yield the victory to you at this time?"

Lord Tsekuin's reply rang out loud enough to raise echoes.

"I do not consent. Let the game continue to the end."

The Hongshu's face turned even whiter. His hand no longer trembled. Instead it looked to Blade as though the man was having to fight an urge to draw his sword and fly at Blade or Lord Tsekuin. Nothing but fear of what he might unleash by sweeping away law and custom like that seemed to be holding him back.

Then the tension that might have flashed into violence and chaos passed. The Hongshu sighed visibly, crossed his arms on his chest, and nodded.

"Then let the game continue."

It took only another fifteen or twenty minutes before the last two *dabuni* of the Hongshu's hand joined their comrades on the floor. Neither really had the nerve left to defend themselves, and Blade didn't feel particularly good about killing either one. He understood why Lord Tsekuin might want to rub the Hongshu's nose in his defeat. But it still seemed like an ugly and meaningless butchery.

Silence returned to the chamber as the last of the Hongshu's fighters gave his death rattle and lay still. Blade was conscious that the Hongshu's eyes were fixed on him more intently than before. Blade raised his spear in the formal salute and waited for the man to speak.

"Blade. It is known to you that your lord is doomed for his crime?"

"It is."

"It is known to you that you will thenceforward be an *uroi*, a *dabuno* without a lord?"

"It is."

"You are a man who came to Gaikon from a distant land. You have no home in Gaikon, save by the grace of a lord whom you serve. I offer you the chance to serve me, to become a *dabuno* sworn to the Hongshu and no other lord."

Now Blade was conscious that Lord Tsekuin and Doifuzan were also staring intently at him. They seemed surprised. This hadn't been part of their plans. Blade smiled thinly. Obviously the Hongshu was trying to salvage "face," if he could salvage nothing else from this shambles. It would take something away from Lord Tsekuin's last victory if he saw the man who had won it for him going over to the Hongshu.

But he wasn't going to see that. Blade knew that the moment he understood the Hongshu's offer. The man was too short-tempered, too treacherous, and too powerful to make a safe master.

Besides, Lord Tsekuin deserved more. Blade honestly couldn't say exactly how much loyalty he felt to the doomed man, doomed by his own folly. But he knew he felt enough to make it impossible for him to serve the Hongshu.

Blade made the deepest and most ceremonial bow. "Noble Hongshu, I must refuse." He bowed again. As he straightened up, he saw Lord Tsekuin and Doifuzan exchange quick, startled glances.

The Hongshu's self-control snapped with an almost audible *craaaak!* He leaped to his feet and screeched, "Serpent and slime! If you will not serve me, then you will serve no one! Every lord in Gaikon will be ordered to refuse your oath, under pain of death—and not the honorable death of Lord Tsekuin either! They will die as rebels if they let you serve them. Try to live in Gaikon for a year or two with no man's hand reaching out to help you, Blade! Then you will come to me, begging on your knees to be allowed to serve me!"

Blade wrinkled up his face as though he smelled something. "Wait and see, noble Hongshu, before you count your victories. The victory counted beforehand may fly away the fastest. This you have seen today, I think."

For a moment it looked as though the Hongshu might drop dead on the spot, or try to kill Blade. A deadly tension was in the air again. Then it passed. The Hongshu clapped his hands, gongs sounded from above, and servants came rushing in to carry away the bodies and Lord Geron on his stretcher.

When the door slid shut behind the Hongshu, Blade turned again to look at Lord Tsekuin and Doifuzan. They were alternately looking at him and at each other. Once more Blade had the impression that they were judging him for a part in some game that would go on outside this chamber—a game in which he would have a part whether he knew the rules or not.

15

Blade knocked lightly three times on the sliding wooden door. The signal would alert Lady Oyasa without carrying warning to any ears that might be listening. There weren't likely to be many in the half-deserted castle in any case. Maids and attendants and servants had been fleeing like frightened birds ever since the return from Deyun a week ago.

From the lady's point of view, that was fine. It made it safe and easy to hold her final rendezvous with Blade in the comfort of a castle chamber, rather than in the drafty hut in the dark woods. The booby traps were disconnected, the eunuchs and maids had fled, and only Lady Musura was standing by.

The panic of Lord Tsekuin's household was a grim spectacle. To Blade the castle seemed like an old man, dying alone and deserted by all his friends. For years it had been a place of safety to those who served Lord Tsekuin. Now they fled as though a volcano was about to erupt underneath it.

Blade didn't blame them. Even some of the *dabuni* had fled into the mountains when word came that the Hungshu's army was approaching, ten thousand strong. They would occupy the castle and lands peacefully if possible. But they would fight if anyone was foolish enough to resist.

So far nobody had been that foolish. They fled or waited for the inevitable. Blade was left alone to prowl the empty halls of the castle, his footsteps echoing hollowly.

The three knocks were repeated from the far side of the door. Then it scraped open. Blade slipped through into darkness, but he heard breathing and a gentle laugh in that darkness. Then a yellow spark flared. An orange yellow glow wavered to life.

"Welcome, Blade. Welcome to our farewell."

Lady Oyasa was already on her sleeping mat and curled up under the quilts. Only her head and bare shoulders were visible. Her black hair was unbound and flowed like a river of ink across the pillows. Blade felt desire rise in him as he looked at her lying there. Desire—and regret. She was right. This would be their farewell, however much longer he found himself staying in Gaikon. He barred the door behind him, laid his swords on the floor, threw off his cloak, and began undoing his sash.

Knowing this was their last time gave the lovemaking something new. Call it tenderness, call it—Blade really didn't care what they called it. He only knew that it was there. He also knew that because of it he went on and on, again and again, and it did the same for Lady Oyasa. She muffled her screams into whimpers and groans. But she gasped, sucked in air as though she were drowning, clawed at Blade's back and shoulders, bit his ears, locked her legs around him, writhed and heaved herself about like a madwoman.

How long they went on, Blade couldn't even guess. Time lost its meaning for both of them. But eventually they both reached the end of their strength. They lay quietly, in luxurious exhaustion, until their panting breath steadied and the sweat dried on their bare skins.

"Blade," said Lady Oyasa. She ran a long-fingered

hand across his chest. "You know I must spend tomorrow night with my husband."

"Yes." The morning of the day after tomorrow was fixed for Lord Tsekuin's suicide. "Custom demands it."

"Yes, and I wish it also. In some ways my husband has been a fool. If he had not been a fool he would not be facing what he now faces. But he had some notions of honor and decency. He has asked my forgiveness for much that he has made me endure. I think that if he were not doomed, we"— She broke off. Blade sensed that she found "what might have been" too painful, and did not press her.

After another silence, she went on. "I think there are also a good many of my husband's *dabuni* who are willing to forgive his faults. But they will not forget the Hongshu's treachery, nor Lord Geron. Yezjaro is young, Doifuzan is old, but I think both have long memories."

"I agree," said Blade. He grinned. "They also both have a talent for keeping their mouths shut. I too suspect they have some plans of their own afoot. But I don't know any more about them than you do."

Lady Oyasa shrugged. "Why should I? I am a woman, and Yezjaro at least suspects that my conduct has not been all that it should be. Besides, I will be returning to my family, and my sister is married to a man too high in the Hongshu's councils for comfort.

"You are a proven and mighty warrior, but you are a stranger in Gaikon. The Hongshu himself offers you a place in his service. In fact, he wishes you in his service so badly that he goes to great lengths to keep you from serving any other lord. Is it surprising that my husband's *dabuni* seem to think you may be tempted? To serve the Hongshu is—"

"They don't know me very well," said Blade sharply. "Even if I owed Lord Tsekuin or his memory no loyalty at all, there is still common sense. I have served many lords in many lands, some stranger by far than Gaikon. If I had not learned to recognize a man too treacherous to follow safely, I would never have lived to reach Gaikon."

"That would have been sad," said Lady Oyasa with a smile. "For many people." Her arms reached out for him again. Blade found that he had no trouble responding.

When the very last fit of passion had faded away, Lady Oyasa reached under her pillow and drew out a small lacquered metal box.

"This is for you, Blade. For all you have done, and for all you may yet do."

Blade unlatched the box, pushed back the lid, and reached inside. Something wrapped in red silk lay there on a piece of fur. He unbound the silk, and stared.

A diamond lay there in the palm of his hand. A diamond of the finest gem quality, expertly cut and faceted into an oval, and at least six hundred carats. Blade tried to compute its value in home dimension terms, then realized he couldn't. No diamond that size had turned up in home dimension for many years. But he was obviously holding several million dollars at least in the palm of his hand.

"I thought of giving you something simply to make you remember me," Lady Oyasa said. "But this is better. It will also stand between you and hunger if necessary." Her lips softly caressed his.

Blade couldn't see any reason to try putting their farewell into words. Instead he rose silently, dressed and armed himself, and slipped out. The lamp went out behind him as he stepped through the doorway, and in the darkness he heard a faint sob. Then Lady Musura seemed to sprout from the floor at his side, sliding the door shut and leading him away down the silent halls.

Lord Tsekuin and Lady Oyasa spent the next night together. Blade spent the next night in the lowest cellars of the castle, carefully disguising the diamond. By the time he had finished the job, the diamond looked and smelled like something dredged up from a particularly filthy sewer. Blade then wrapped it in silk again and coated the silk with hot wax to keep the smell in and prying fingers out. Lady Oyasa had been right. The diamond could be his fortune. It could even more easily get him a slit throat if anyone knew he had it.

Morning came. Before the dew had dried on the sand of the courtyard the *dabuni* who were to witness Lord Tsekuin's death had assembled. Blade was among them. Yezjaro and Doifuzan might have their doubts about Blade's loyalty, but they would not give him the mortal insult of barring him from Lord Tsekuin's last ritual.

The sun rose above the roofs surrounding the courtyard. Lord Tsekuin appeared, dressed in white from head to foot, his feet bare and his head shaved and annointed with the oil of Kunkoi. The priestess followed him, and after the priestess came a servant, carrying a short sword with a particularly ornate hilt.

Lord Tsekuin knelt on a small square of black silk that contrasted sharply with the white sand spread across the courtyard. The priestess hobbled three times around him in a circle, intoning blessings to speed his spirit to the Sun Goddess as it deserved.

Then from opposite sides Doifuzan and the servant stepped forward. The servant handed Lord Tsekuin the short sword. Doifuzan drew his own sword and took a solid two-handed grip on it. A deathly silence fell on the courtyard.

Lord Tsekuin raised the short sword, then turned it in his hand until it was pointing at the right side of his stomach. His mouth hardened into a thin line. Then with a jerk of his arm he drove the point of the sword into himself.

His face twisted, but his hand locked on the sword, driving it in deeper. He coughed, and blood sprayed from his mouth, leaving spots on the sand and on his white clothing. Then he began to draw the sword across his stomach, leaving a gaping bloody slash.

As he finished carving the slash, Doifuzan stepped forward. The first *dabuno's* sword flashed in the sun, then whistled down in an arc. Lord Tsekuin's head leaped from his shoulders in a mighty fountaining spray of blood and fell to the sand with a dull *whump*. The headless body remained kneeling upright for a moment. Then it folded forward and lay motionless as the last few beats of the heart drove out the last of the blood. The smell of the blood rose thickly into the warm still air of the courtyard.

Doifuzan raised one hand. "It is finished, and our lord has done his duty to the Hongshu."

Yezjaro stepped forward and also raised one hand. "Let us be mindful of our duty also." Blade tried to catch the instructor's eyes, but the young man refused to meet Blade's gaze. He persistently looked away, until Blade finally gave up, turned away, and strode off toward the gate of the courtyard. No one followed him, spoke to him, or even looked at his departing back.

16

Blade left the castle as soon as he could. A few days' food, extra clothes and footgear, the diamond, and a couple of knives filled a sack slung over one shoulder. His two swords rode in place in his sash, and the best spear he could find in the armory rode on the other shoulder.

No one bothered him as he equipped himself or as he walked to the castle gate. No one spoke to him, even to curse him. But a few of the *dabuni* he passed could not conceal the doubt in their eyes as they looked at him. He was a man who had been invited to join the service of the Hongshu. How could he not be tempted? How could he be trusted to be faithful to the end to Lord Tsekuin's memory?

Blade wasn't going to worry about these vague suspicions. But he wanted to be well away from the castle before the suspicions turned into open hostility. That hostility could too easily inspire someone with the idea of sticking a knife into Blade some dark night. He was damned if he was going to let this whole frustrating mission in Gaikon end in such an ignominious death!

A mile beyond the gate he met the advanced guard of the Hongshu's army moving in on the castle. The elaborately armored mounted officer in command hailed him.

"You are the stranger, Blade, are you not?"

Blade nodded silently.

"Then I have a message for you." He reached into a pouch at his belt, drew out a scroll, and tossed it arrogantly. "Open it and read, Blade." His voice was harsh and gloating.

Blade felt more like unlimbering his spear and ramming about two feet of it up into the officers' belly. But he clamped down on his temper and obeyed.

The scroll was simple and blunt. The *dabuno* Blade, from lands outside Gaikon and formerly in the service of Lord Tsekuin, was under suspicion of plotting against the Hongshu. He was not yet worthy of confinement or interrogation, but no warlords might swear him into their service. He was to keep this scroll on his person at all times and in all places and show it to any officer or lord who might ask. Failure to do so would lead to his immediate arrest.

It was signed by Lord Geron.

After reading that, Blade felt even more like removing at least one officer from the Hungshu's service. But there were at least fifty armed men within a few yards, some of them archers. This was not the time or the place.

Instead he bowed. "The Hongshu has spoken," he intoned.

"He has," said the officer. "I hope some day you will listen to him more respectfully."

Blade bowed again. "Not bloody likely!" was the reply in his mind as he strode away down the road.

The next few weeks were about the most frustrating in Blade's whole life. Lord Tsekuin was dead, so Blade's place in Gaikon as a member of Tsekuin's household was gone. The household itself was scattered and the castle and lands swarming with the Hongshu's troops. Some of the *dabuni* were obviously planning something to avenge their dead lord. But none of them would say a word to Blade. He suspected that some of them might kill him for even asking. There seemed to be nothing for him to do but wander off and spend the rest of his time in Gaikon exploring the land. Sooner or later, Lord Leighton's computer would snatch him back to home dimension, scroll, diamond, and all. No doubt the diamond would be put to good use—it was worth enough to finance the whole Project Dimension X for months. But that seemed about all he was going to get out of this particular trip.

But wandering through Gaikon was not as easy as Blade had hoped. Not while he carried the Hongshu's scroll. If he had been able to disguise himself, he might have been able to safely throw it away. But his light skin could not easily be disguised, and that set him apart. Even under a coat of dirt it remained suspiciously pale. So he kept the scroll, showed it when asked, and roamed the land as a law-abiding *uroi*, a masterless *dabuno*.

After the first weary weeks of tramping the roads in all weathers and at all hours, Blade began to drift toward Deyun. The Hongshu's capital might not be the safest place for a man in his position, but it would certainly be a more comfortable place to wait out the rest of his time in Gaikon than some drafty peasant hut in a mountain village. There would be people who knew what was going on. There would be women. There might even be some of Lord Tsekuin's *dabuni*, particuarly Yezjaro.

If there were any of those, Blade was going to ask a few questions. He made up his mind that he was also going to get answers, whether the people he asked were willing to give them or not. He might not owe Lord Tsekuin the deep loyalty that the other *dabuni* felt, but treachery like the Hongshu's disgusted him. If he could help make the ruler pay, he would.

Besides, he still didn't like being left out of things.

Deyun seemed even bigger and more crowded than Blade remembered it. But as he had expected, it was easier to live there. There were usually men and women who would stand an *uroi* a drink or a meal or a night's lodging. The ones who learned that Blade had served Lord Tsekuin were particularly generous. None of them said anything precise, out of fear of the Hongshu's informers. But none of them left Blade in any doubt that they thought Lord Tsekuin had been sadly abused.

Not that there was much hope of any rebellion succeeding. At least fifty thousand of the Hongshu's soldiers were quartered in and around Deyun. Two or three times as many appeared to be scattered in garrisons all over Gaikon. It wasn't surprising that even those who might hate and fear the Hongshu weren't willing to risk the price involved in rebelling against him.

The fact that Deyun was swarming with the Hongshu's soldiers and officials soon began to give Blade problems. The Hongshu's men seemed to have orders to do everything they could think of to make Blade's life impossible.

First it was stopping him five and six times a day to check if he still had his scroll. Then it was searching him, more to annoy him than with the idea of finding anything. They fingered the package holding the diamond, but never tried to open it.

The next step was parties of soldiers stopping in at taverns where Blade might be having a meal. They yelled curses, bullied the servants, broke furniture, threw cups and plates around, drove off the other customers, and generally made nuisances of themselves and a mess of the place.

The climax came when twelve soldiers stormed into a tavern where Blade was sipping wine and filling himself with fish and porridge. They upset the stove.

They broke all the wine jugs and poured the wine on the hot coals. They slashed the scrolls on the walls with their swords. They knocked the tavernkeeper down and kicked him in the stomach and ribs until he was writhing and coughing blood. They snatched his daughter from where she cowered in a back room and threw her down on the mats. Then all twelve of them raped her there on the floor. Her screams drew an angry crowd. The crowd swiftly drew more soldiers, too many for Blade to fight. He suspected also that if he fought anyway, the soldiers would massacre everybody in the crowd. Although he was white and shakiing with rage, he couldn't see what else there was to do but quietly slip away.

Word of the incident spread rapidly. Within a few days Blade found that he was no longer welcome in most shops and taverns in Deyun. People did not hate him—their voices shook with rage when they mentioned the Hongshu. But they turned him away nonetheless.

Blade found himself having to offer to work for his keep. But no one dared to risk hiring him as a guard or a house servant. Those who hired him for menial jobs knew that he was desperate, and paid him as little as they dared. Sometimes his pay for a day's hard work was nothing more than a bowl of porridge and a few sour vegetables.

After a few days of this Blade was about ready to leave Deyun behind and head out into the country again. If he stayed in the city and refused to join the Hongshu's service, sooner or later he would starve or have to turn thief. He might still have to turn bandit out in the country. But at least there he would be farther from the Hongshu's soldiers, and so have a better chance to return safely to home dimension. That was about all he could hope for now. The trip to Gaikon had been a waste almost from first to last.

He decided to wait one more day, then head for the country. Then he rose and went out into the morning.

He was walking along a street about a mile from the Warm Gates quarter when he heard harsh, angry voices from ahead. They came from a small alley off to the right. Blade quickened his step, but did not draw his sword or unsling his spear—yet.

A few steps took him to the entrance to the alley. A middle-aged woman in peasant clothing was backed against the sooty timbers of one side of the alley. At her feet lay a large bundle of rushes. She was holding out both hands in front of her, trying to fend off four soldiers who were trying to push her back against the wall and clutch at her trousers.

Blade's temper flared. He had been willing to put up with a lot from the Hongshu's soldiers as long as he had some good reason. But now he could leave Deyun any time he wanted to. Why not do something about at least a few of those swaggering thugs before he left?

Why not indeed?

Blade swung his spear off his shoulder, grasped it with both hands, and stepped forward into the alley. His voice boomed out. "Stop that, you vomit-weaned sons of diseased pigs!"

The soldiers turned to stare at Blade. So did the woman. Then Blade stopped for a moment to stare at her. The long straight nose, the small firm chin, the thinly disguised pattern of scars on the right side of her face—he recognized them all.

It was Lady Musura.

17

In the same moment, Lady Musura recognized Blade. The knowledge that she had an ally seemed to pull a trigger in her. She exploded into savage action. A foot shot up and out, into one soldier's unprotected groin. He screamed and reeled back, bumping into one of his comrades. The two men became tangled for a moment, leaving an opening in the half-circle around the *jinai* woman. She leaped high, flipping head over heels in midair, drawing a knife as she flew and landing beside Blade, facing the other two soldiers.

One of them drew his sword and charged, mindlessly, like a wild boar. Blade's spear point drove into the wrist of the man's sword hand, tearing flesh, smashing bone apart. A flick of Blade's wrist shifted the spear, sending it into the man's throat.

The other soldier came on in a crouch. Blade's arms jerked and the spear shaft smashed into the side of the man's neck. He reeled and crumpled forward onto his knees. Lady Musura darted in and both her hands slashed in under his jaw. His breath became a choked gurgle as bone fragments clogged his throat, and he collapsed.

By this time the third soldier had decided to throw courage to the winds. He dropped his spear and took to his heels. The soldier Lady Musura had kicked in the groin took off after him, but he was too bent over with pain to get out of range in time. The lady's knife sang through the air and into the back of the soldier's neck. He sprawled full length on the smelly cobblestones of the alley.

Blade leaped forward over the dying men and snatched up the fallen spear. One rule he always followed in a fight: never miss a chance to pick up a spare weapon. As he slung it over his shoulder, Lady Musura grabbed at his sleeve and stared up into his face. Her eyes were wide and her face pale under its tan and grime, but her voice was as steady as ever.

"Blade, I thank you. But it would have been wiser not to do this."

"Maybe. But I was tired of those damned soldiers pushing me and everybody else around."

"A good thought, but perhaps better for some other time and place. Now we must flee."

"I was leaving the city anyway, tomorrow. We can—"

The distant but angry booming of a gong interrupted Blade. He frowned. "An alarm? So soon?"

"Yes. We have no hope of leaving the city now or for many days. We must flee to the quarter of the Warm Gates. The courtesans there are always searching for people to guard their houses, and no one would turn us over to the Hongshu's soldiers."

"Not if they could help it. But if the Hongshu has fifty thousand soliders in Deyun—"

"He will not dare send one of them through the Warm Gates without the leave of the courtesans. Interrupt the business of that quarter for even a single night, and there will be rioting and burning enough to make even the Hongshu uncertain on his throne. Besides, there are a few of the ladies and masters in that quarter who owe me favors from years past. They would hide us no matter what."

The sound of the gongs was mixing with angry shouts as they stepped out of the alley into the open street. In spite of this, they walked as slowly as possible, trying to look like peaceful citizens going about their business.

The disguise gained them a few valuable minutes, as they made their way slowly through the tangle of streets toward the Warm Gates. Several parties of soldiers pounded past at a run, shoving citizens up against walls and into doorways, upsetting stands and carts, knocking peddlers off their feet. Blade even stopped once to help a fish peddler pick up his baskets and listen to him roundly cursing the soldiers.

They covered more than half the distance to the Warm Gates in less than ten minutes. But then the streets began to narrow. The crowds grew thicker and harder to push through. Several times they had to cut through dark, narrow, foul-smelling alleys, stumbling over rotten vegetables, slimy mud puddles, long-dead cats and dogs.

Their luck ran out as they came out of their fourth alley, not more than a hundred yards from the Warm Gates. Between them and the gates a line of soldiers blocked the street as solidly as a wall. The sun glinted on their armor, and above them sprouted a forest of spearpoints and helmet spikes and horns. Blade froze and tried to fade back into the darkness of the alley. Before he could do so, someone in the line of soliders shouted:

"There they are!"

Blade's sword flew clear. He drew his short sword too, and tossed it to Lady Musura. Then they darted out into the street, heading toward the wall of the Warm Gates quarter.

There were archers among the soldiers. If they had simply stood back and let fly, Blade and Lady Musura wouldn't have covered ten feet. But perhaps there were enough citizens around to make even the Hongshu's cold-blooded soldiers careful. Or more likely they all had notions of winning glory by killing or capturing the mighty Blade themselves, sword against sword.

The line broke apart as the soldiers began pushing their way toward the two fugitives. Men cursed, women screamed, children squalled in pain and terror as the soldiers used fists and spear butts. Then the crowd also broke apart as people tried to flatten themselves against the wall or run. Blade and Lady Musura found themselves caught in a logjam of people all pushing and heaving frantically. In desperation they used their own fists and elbows, struggling furiously to stay on their feet and move even a few steps toward the wall. Blade felt as though his ribs would cave in, tried to keep the points of his spears out of a child's face, stumbled over a smashed cart, and nearly went down. Sweat streamed down his face, making streaks in the dust on his skin. He couldn't help thinking that being trampled to death in a panic-stricken mob was a stinking way to go out.

Then he and the *jinai* woman were as much out in the open as they could be, in a little niche formed by a buttress of the wall. At the same moment five soldiers broke out of the crowd. Blade swung one of his spears down and threw it at the leader. It took him in the groin. Clawing at the shaft, he went over backward. The other four drew their swords, but hesitated for a moment.

Lady Musura used that moment to leap catlike onto the wall. Her supple fingers and toes seemed to find holds where Blade would have suspected nothing but blank stone. She swarmed up to the top of the wall. Blade flashed a glare at her. Was she deserting him now, when—?

Before he could finish the thought, she called down, "Hold on, Blade! What I need I must find within." She vanished down inside the wall. Blade swore under his breath. He hoped she was telling the truth. But whether she was or not, there was no reason to lie down and die. If he was going to finish it here, he would take some more of those stinking soldiers with him!

One of the soldiers screwed up his courage and leaped forward, sword high and flashing. Blade brought up his own sword and the remaining spear to guard. Then he noticed the man's clumsy positioning. Almost effortlessly Blade's spear licked out, driving into the shoulder of the man's sword arm. His fingers opened and let the sword fall. Before it clattered to the street Blade's own sword hissed down. The man's other arm flew from its shoulder. Blood sprayed the man's comrades. His howl of agony drowned out even the roar of the panic-stricken crowd.

Blade followed up his edge with a quick attack. He dropped his sword, used a two-handed grip to push the spear into the face of the next soldier, and grounded the spear. The sword leaped into his hand again, in time to meet the last two soldiers as they came in together. One swung so wildly that his sword whistled down over Blade's head and clanged against the stone. Before the man could pull back his half-numbed arm, Blade drove his short sword into the man's armpit.

That left only one soldier facing Blade. But five or six more were pushing through the crowd, ready to join in the fight. Blade knew he would have to be quick with this man.

But either the soldier was naturally cautious or the fate of his comrades had put caution into him. He stayed well out of Blade's reach, bobbing and ducking under Blade's slashes. He might not be a very good swordsman, and he certainly wouldn't have lasted more than moments against Yezjaro. But he was good enough to keep clear of Blade's sword for a minute or two. Finally he missed a step, Blade's sword sank into his neck, his head lolled helplessly—and seven of his comrades burst through the crowd to confront Blade.

As they did Blade heard something hit the ground behind him with a soft thud. One of the soldiers pointed upward, shouted in alarm—then screamed as one of Lady Musura's knives sprouted in his left eye. Blade turned and saw a thin rope trailing down the wall and Lady Musura crouching on top.

One leap took Blade five feet up the wall. His hands locked on the rope. It bit into his hands until he could feel the blood oozing, but it held his weight. He ignored the pain and hauled himself swiftly upward. One of the soldiers dashed in and aimed a cut at Blade, leaping high to deliver it. Blade felt a puff of air on his ankle as the sword flashed by, and climbed even faster.

His head and shoulders were just clear of the top of the wall when the first arrows smacked into the wall beside him. He knew the soldiers must be too confused for accurate shooting. Otherwise their first volley would have been enough. But his luck would still run out if he hung here long enough. He slapped his hands down flat on the top of the wall and sent himself flying upward and over.

Too late he saw what lay below him on the other side. More arrows whistled overhead as he plunged down, to land flat on his belly in eight feet of cold, scummy water. A fearful smell of unnameable things much too long dead rose around Blade as his head broke the scum. He spat out the scum, fought down an urge to vomit—then was submerged in another wave of muck as Lady Musura landed beside him in the moat.

"First time I've ever seen a moat inside the castle walls," he said, trying to smile.

Lady Musura removed a long string of something mercifully unidentifiable from her hair and smiled back. "Oh, there are many strange things about the hospitality of those of the quarter of the Warm Gates."

Outside the walls the angry roar of soldiers' voices and the shouted orders of their officers were rising to drown out the crowd noises. Then from down by the Warm Gates themselves Blade heard the unmistakable thud and boom of many fists and spear butts hammering on wood.

Blade couldn't help wondering. Would he and Lady Musura still receive the hospitality of the quarter if it involved making a stand against the Hongshu's whole army?

18

The hospitality of the Warm Gates quarter held firm against the Hongshu's soldiers. But this was not entirely a matter of the stubbornness of the courtesans or their debts to Lady Musura. It was not even a matter of the soldiers' arrows having killed and wounded several people within the quarter.

News that the soldiers were trying to break into the Warm Gates quarter spread swiftly through Deyun. Within an hour the soldiers at the gates were hemmed in by a mob at least ten thousand strong. More soldiers appeared to disperse the crowd. Fighting started between the soldiers and some of the tougher citizens—porters, sailors, bargemen. Within two hours a tremendous riot was raging through the streets around the Warm Gates quarter. Curses, shouts, screams of fear and agony filled the air. Then came sounds of splintering wood and crackling flames as overturned stoves set fire to mats and paper partitions.

Eventually somebody in authority gathered his wits together and called off the soldiers. He was just in time. From the roof of a building inside the walls, Blade could see the riot spreading slowly but surely across the city. If it went on much longer, the Hongshu might have a full-scale revolt on his hands. That would certainly be one way of avenging Lord Tsekuin and teaching the ruler of Gaikon a badly needed lesson. But Blade didn't much care for getting thousands of innocent people killed in the process.

He wanted to deliver the message to the Hongshu more personally. He suspected that the *dabuni* who were plotting to avenge their betrayed lord had similar notions.

By dusk the riot had burned itself out, and so had many of the fires started during the rioting. But others went on burning through the night, sending up clouds of smoke and a sinister red glare over the quarter. By dawn only smoking debris remained of nearly a dozen streets.

Standing with Lady Musura on the roof of the same building, Blade inhaled the cool morning air and looked out over the city. In the distance he could see the dark, sprawling mass of the Hongshu's palace.

Lady Musura rested a hand on his shoulder and followed his eyes with her own.

"You think again, perhaps, of striking back, for Lord Tsekuin's memory?"

Blade nodded. "There was a time when I didn't see any point in trying. If the *dabuni* did not trust me, so be it. But now—now I think I am angry enough to want to strike at the Hongshu alone, if necessary." It was almost his last chance before returning to home dimension to make his whole journey to Gaikon worthwhile. Blade did not want to see an entire journey into Dimension X wasted.

"You will not be alone," said Lady Musura. Her hand reached out and clasped his. "I will stand beside you in everything you may wish or seek to do. My eyes will be your eyes, my lips your lips, my sword your sword."

Blade turned to look down at the woman beside him.

"You once served the Hongshu as a *jinai*. What makes you turn against him now?" He did not want to have to add, "What makes you think I should trust you not to betray me and any others who may join us?"

Lady Musura was silent for a long moment. "I swore an oath to serve the Hongshu until released and never lift a weapon against him. I have been released, and I will not forswear the second part of my oath even now. Do you think even Yezjaro and Doifuzan wish to strike at the Hongshu himself, and let loose chaos in Gaikon?"

"Not if they are wise."

"Then assume I am wise also. Our blow will—must—fall on Lord Geron. We know whose orders he obeys, to be sure. But the words that drove Lord Tsekuin to rage and folly were spoken by Lord Geron. Lord Geron's death will go far to avenge Lord Tsekuin. It will also be a warning to the Hongshu. Perhaps he will think twice the next time he plots against a warlord, if he considers that it may cost him trusted servants. Diamond mines are often easier to find than second chancellors who will obey in silence."

Blade nodded. He could not have described the situation more accurately himself.

The fact that Blade and Lady Musura were now working as a team toward a common goal didn't immediately work any miracles. Their work as guards in the quarter left them a good deal of free time, but information still came slowly for them.

Lord Geron, they soon discovered, was still convalescing at his private house inside the palace walls. Between Lord Geron and any possible assassins stood the mazes, traps, and guards of the great palace. Those guards were picked fighting men, unlike the soldiers Blade had killed in the streets.

But Lady Musura had been a *jinai* of the

Hongshu's service. Perhaps she knew her way through the mazes to Lord Geron's house?

She shook her head when Blade asked her that. "The traps and passwords are changed every few months. I know nothing of what might have been done in the four years since I was last within the palace. Even if I could guide you, we would be only two. Any accident could doom us. We must go in force when we go. That means more men than could ever pass unobserved through the mazes."

Obviously the Hongshu made sure that even those who ferreted out other's secrets for him did not ferret out his. Blade could recognize security-consciousness when he saw it. He could also curse it, when it stood between him and his goals.

But now memories awoke, memories of what Yezjaro had once said about secret routes for bringing Warm Gates ladies into the Hongshu's palace for the delight of the nobles. Those memories had slept since he had heard the instructor's words. Why not, when until now there had been no prospect of ever doing anything with them?

He told Lady Musura. She lit up with delight. "Yes, I remember now. I never had anything to do with it myself. But several of the *jinai* I knew were once put to work spying on just that."

"What did they find out?"

"They did not speak of it in detail. But it was decided that there was no danger to the Hongshu from it. I think no one tried to stop it."

"Good. Did you learn the names of any of the Warm Gates people involved?"

"No. Even if I had, much would have changed since then. But I am sure that we can learn if we work quietly. I doubt if the hospitality of the quarter would be ours for long if they learned what we were planning."

"That will take time," said Blade.

"I know," said Lady Musura. "But it seems the best thing we can do for our lord."

Blade nodded. He was also happy that Lady Musura knew the matter was going to take time. If there was one thing he had learned in his home dimension espionage work, it was to give a project all the time it needed. Shortcuts were too often shortcuts to disaster. Two people working alone against the ruler of Gaikon couldn't afford even the smallest accident.

In a week they knew that the smuggling of Warm Gates ladies into the palace was still going on. But it took a month more before they had learned the route, with its underground passages, concealed stairs, and the rest.

Lady Musura, an expert at disguises, worked by day. Blade, his skin finally darkened by dye Lady Musura concocted, worked by night. They slept little, ate less, grew gaunt and tired, seldom spoke about anything but their latest discoveries. But it was a satisfying time for both of them. Lady Musura was working to avenge Lord Tsekuin and strike a blow against the Hongshu. Blade was doing the same, and he was also working with a fellow professional in the deadly but exhilarating game of espionage.

Eventually the job was done as well as it could be done. They sat in their tiny back room one evening, drinking the first jug of *saya* they had allowed themselves in weeks. A small charcoal stove burned in one corner, filling the air with pungent gray smoke and driving some of the chill out of the air. The year was wearing on. They would do well to strike soon.

"We can't wait much longer, Blade," said Lady Musura. "I know of a certainty that the Hongshu keeps spies within the quarter. Sooner or later it will be known in the palace that we have learned what we have learned. Then a trap will be laid for us, or for anyone else coming through. Assassins may even enter the quarter, striking us down when we think we are safe."

"I know," said Blade. It was one of the classic problems in espionage. Ideally you should move as soon as possible after learning what you need, before the enemy learns that you have penetrated his secrets. But there are always practical problems.

"Two people aren't going to be enough, unless Lord Geron's guards are all too drunk to keep any sort of watch. Even if we could overcome the guards, we might not be able to keep Lord Geron from escaping. It would be a gesture, nothing more. I don't want to waste what we've learned on a gesture."

"No more I," said Lady Musura. "But where in the name of Kunkoi can we find—?" She broke off, and her eyes widened. "You think we should send word to the other *dabuni*?"

Blade nodded. "I think we would owe it to them even if we did not need their help. Do you doubt that Yezjaro and Doifuzan have plans for avenging Lord Tsekuin's death on Lord Geron?"

"None. But will they trust us or follow our lead or even listen to us?"

"I wish I could be sure. But I think Yezjaro will at least listen to me until I have told him everything."

"Possibly. But where is Yezjaro?"

"We will have to find him."

"That may take time, Blade. We may not have any more time."

"I know. But have we any other choice?"

19

At first, it looked like finding Yezjaro would be like finding a single fish in the ocean. But Blade knew that the young instructor was too fond of wine, warmth, and women to drift away to some mountain warlord's castle. If he was still alive, he was likely to be close enough to Deyun so that they would hear of him sooner rather than later. But how much time did they have?

The waiting became an ordeal. Blade knew that patience was essential in this game. But he also knew that if he spent much more time sitting in the cramped back room, he might take out his bad temper on Lady Musura.

So he took to drifting through the taverns by day as well as by night. Within a week, he had drifted straight into what he was looking for.

Two *dabuni* wandered into a tavern where Blade was sitting over *saya* and biscuits, ordered their own wine, and began to talk.

"Poor stupid Kuras," said one. "He wouldn't believe the 'Flying Bird Cut' could do all that Yezjaro said it could."

"No great blame there," said the other. "Why should anyone take it on faith?"

"He shouldn't, I agree. But to insult Yezjaro to his face was the act of a fool."

"Well, he paid for it. And not as heavily as he

deserved, either. Yezjaro used a wooden sword, so Kuras will live even if he won't walk again."

Blade rose and went over to the two *dabuni*. "Excuse me, Honorable *Dabuni*, but are you speaking of Yezjaro, master of the 'Flying Bird Cut'?"

One of the *dabuni* glared at Blade and started to answer him contemptuously, then noticed Blade's size and the two swords in his sash. His face straightened itself out and he replied more coolly, "Yes, I am. He stays now at our lord's house, near the city. What would you want with him?"

"I would have you take a message to him," said Blade. "If he will come to this tavern tomorrow night at the tenth hour, the man whom he would need ten minutes to defeat would speak with him."

"Is there such a man?" said the first *dabuno*, with a harsh laugh. "I cannot imagine it."

"Whether there is or not, I do not know," said Blade politely. "But a man whom Yezjaro once described as such would like to speak to him."

"Must Yezjaro come alone?" said the second *dabuno*. His eyes were fixed on Blade, hard and skeptical.

"That is as the Honorable Instructor wishes," said Blade. It would be far better if Yezjaro did come alone. But mentioning that to these two men would probably make them suspect treachery. In any case, Yezjaro would be certain to recognize the message. There had been no one else within earshot the day he praised Blade's swordsmanship with those words.

"Anything will be as the master wishes," said the first *dabuno*. "Including your death, if this is a trap."

Blade bowed politely. He was still bowing politely as he backed out of the tavern, and he did not straighten up with a sigh of relief until he was out in the street. At least he had found his fish. That was a good beginning.

Yezjaro appeared at the tavern at the appointed time the next evening. He came alone, as Blade had expected. The instructor might wonder who was asking for him, in spite of the message. But he was too proud and too self-confident to admit that there was any situation in which he might need help.

That was not good sense. But there was a gallantry in it that Blade could not help admiring. Home dimension offered too few opportunities for it these days. The gallant were too often the first to die, the last to be recognized, and the ones most frequently laughed at.

Yezjaro stalked into the tavern like a tiger on the prowl, light-footed and with one hand close to his sword hilt. He was thinner than he had been a few months ago, and there were dark circles under the deep-set eyes that searched the room from ceiling beams to floor mats. But his robe was as expensive and elegant as ever, his sandals were new, his scabbard polished until its blackness shimmered like metal.

His eyes swung across the tables, reached Blade—and stopped. He blinked twice, and Blade saw his free hand clench tightly into a fist. Those few signs were enough for Blade. He knew he had been recognized.

Blade threw a glance at the door and rose. Yezjaro nodded, turned, and preceded Blade out of the tavern. They stayed well apart as they moved down the noisy Street of the Pink Ape, until they reached a small alley behind a warehouse.

There they stood and faced each other, shielded from prying eyes and ears. Yezjaro spoke first.

"What words do you have for me, Blade? Have you found the Hongshu's service so uncongenial so soon?"

"I have never been in the Hongshu's service, Yezjaro," said Blade. His voice was cool but not hostile. If Yezjaro wanted to play a few games in order to reassure himself, so be it. "And this you should know well enough to have no need of asking me foolish questions."

"Are they foolish questions, Blade? Certainly your former comrades in the service of Lord Tsekuin have seen and heard little of you these past few months. You could have sprouted wings and a green tail for all we knew."

"Indeed?" said Blade. "I thought my departure from among you was *your* wish, not mine. I saw written on every face the clear message: 'Go away, Blade. The Hongshu has tempted you and we fear you must yield sooner or later.' Well, I have not yielded. I think I am farther along in my plans to avenge our foully betrayed lord than you people are in yours."

Yezjaro's eyes narrowed suspiciously and he rested his right hand with elaborate casualness on his sword hilt. "You think there are plans afoot among those who served Lord Tsekuin?"

"My friend, I don't think so. I *know* it. If not, why keep me so much in the dark about what you *dabuni* were going to do? If you were all going to go off and set up cucumber farms in the Wishru Montains, then Kunkoi knows you had no need to keep it a secret! In fact, you would have done well to tell everything to one you suspected might carry tales to the Hongshu. But you said nothing. You obviously feared the kind of tales I might bear."

Yezjaro seemed to be fighting to control his face. When he had won the struggle, he crossed his arms on his chest and frowned at Blade.

"Have you told the Hongshu anything of what you think of us?"

Blade was tempted to smile sarcastically. But he decided it would be better to feign anger, or at least indignation. His voice hardened. "I have already said once that I do not serve the Hongshu. What my eyes see and my ears hear stops with me. It does not go onward to the Hongshu or any who serve him. This makes twice that you have accused me of lacking the honor of a *dabuno* who once served Lord Tsekuin. I will not answer your next accusation with words." He shifted his own right hand to the hilt of his sword.

A long silence fell down between the two men like a stone wall. Blade was tempted to step back, but knew Yezjaro might take that as preparation for an attack. He was also tempted to say something to prod Yezjaro into an answer, but decided against it. The instructor was no fool. As long as he could salvage his pride, he would find no trouble in reaching the correct decision.

Finally the silence was broken. "So, Blade," said Yezjaro. "What are *your* plans for a blow at the Hongshu's pet wolf?"

"We have found a way into his cage, Lady Musura and I," began Blade. He quickly sketched out what they had done and were planning to do. Yezjaro listened in frozen silence. Only his widening eyes and quickening breath showed that he was still living.

"But the two of us cannot strike a blow that will go home," Blade concluded. "There is no wisdom in throwing away our lives to make a mere gesture. Lord Geron must die. For that we thought it proper to call upon those who were once our comrades in the service of the lord we would all avenge. We trust in your honor, though you have not trusted in ours. We ask that your strength and skill be thrown into the battle beside us. If it can be so, then soon we will have Lord Geron's head to cast before the emperor as a lesson for unruly rulers and their servants."

Blade needed to catch his breath after that burst of rhetoric. But he did not take his eyes off Yezjaro, who once again stood silent and motionless. Both fists were clenched now, pale in the darkness.

Blade decided that it was time for the grand gesture. He reached into the pouch that held the diamond and drew out a tightly folded piece of thin paper.

"Honorable Instructor," he said. "At much expense of time and risk of our lives, Lady Musura and I have learned all that we needed to make this. It is a map of the tunnels into the palace, especially to the house of Lord Geron. With it is all other information needed to enter the house and take Lord Geron's head."

Blade held out the map. Mechanically Yezjaro's hand rose to take it and close on it. The instructor's eyes met Blade's. Blade continued. "I ask nothing in return for this. Lady Musura and I trust in the honor of those who served Lord Tsekuin, that they will permit us to take our part in the avenging of his death upon Lord Geron."

"I understand," said Yezjaro tonelessly. Blade would have liked to hear more from the instructor. But that seemed hopeless. Yezjaro looked half stunned and totally speechless. They could not afford to spend much more time out here, where unfriendly eyes and ears might pass by.

"So be it," said Blade. "This is not a matter I can ask you to decide here on the spot. But when a decision has come forth, let word be sent to the House of the Twelve Lanterns on the Street of the Silver Dragon. From there it will reach us swiftly, and we will know what to do after that."

He did not add how much he hoped the *dabuni* would admit him and Lady Musura to their plans. That would be showing a weakness. Instead, he turned away in silence, leaving the instructor standing in the darkness. But as he turned, Blade could not help wondering why he had become so deeply determined to have Lord Geron's head. That determination went far beyond what he might feel for simply getting rid of a dishonest or tyrannical ruler. Was *he* beginning to think according to Gaikon's standards of honor?

Lady Musura was curled up on her sleeping mat in her corner of their dingy little back room by the time Blade returned. The stub of a single candle had almost burned out, leaving a haze of sour-smelling smoke in the room.

Lady Musura awoke as Blade came in. She sat up and lit a second candle as he dropped his swords to the mats and began undressing in silence. Her eyes seemed to be glowing brightly with an unexpected inner light.

"Yezjaro came?"

"He did."

"You gave him the copy of the map?"

"I did."

"Did he say anything?"

"Very little."

"Nothing to show what he will decide?"

"Not a word. I think he appreciates the trust we have shown in his honor. But if this will lead him along the right path—I don't know. I don't even know when we will know."

"Well, then, there's no need for you to stand there grinding your teeth." Lady Musura laughed. "Come and sit down beside me, Blade, and tell me tales of your travels. Do you realize how little we really know of each other, considering how much we have done together?"

Blade dropped his robe to the floor and sat down in his breechclout. Lady Musura lay down again, resting her head on one raised hand. Her eyes, still with the strange light in them, roamed up and down Blade's massive body.

For weeks now Blade had found it easy to think of Lady Musura as a woman, when he wanted to. But they had been working too hard for him to want to more than once or twice. Tonight—well, for the first time in many weeks matters were out of both their hands.

Lady Musura's large eyes seemed to penetrate Blade's skin and read his thoughts. One slender arm crept out from under the quilt and a long-fingered hand began to trace patterns on Blade's bare thigh. He turned to look down at her. Those lips that he had once thought unappealingly thin creased in a smile. Blade bent down and touched those lips with his own. They flowered open, warm, wet, quivering. Then a small supple tongue crept out and flicked back and forth across Blade's own lips.

Lady Musura's hands rose to creep around and caress the small of Blade's back. He thrust his own arms down, drawing Lady Musura up against his body. His hands slipped in under the robe she was wearing, caressing the warm, taut skin stretched over the supple muscles. Her gentle curves felt beautiful to Blade's exploring hands.

His hands crept up from the slim waist to cup the small breasts and feel her nipples harden against his palms. He heard warm breath hissing in his ear. A hand crept from his back around to his stomach, then down into his groin. He became more aware than before of a swollen stiffness down there. Lady Musura's unexpected warmth and softness were drawing their response from him.

Lady Musura twisted to one side, heaving the quilt off the mat onto the floor. Blade stood for a moment to throw off his breechclout, then knelt beside the woman as she quickly flung away her last garment and lay back. Her finely muscled legs drifted apart as Blade's hand stroked the patch of damp black hair between them. Her hands rose again and clutched at Blade's hair, pulling him down until his lips could circle first one nipple, then the other.

But Blade's hands kept up their work while his lips did theirs. His hands alone were enough to bring the woman to her first peak. A quick shudder, a quicker twisting of the small neat head on its slender neck, a whimper and moan deep in her throat.

The sight and sound pushed Blade's own desire even higher. He lifted himself on his hands, held himself there for a moment as Lady Musura shifted under him, then sank down, deep into her. He felt her warmth and wetness take him in, saw her eyes open wide at the feeling of him inside her, heard his own gasp.

Then he was rising and falling deep within her, and Lady Musura was thrusting her hips up toward him to take him in and in and in. His groin became one hot, glorious, delicious agony, that he knew would explode in the next minute. But the next minute came and went, and the minute after that, and still more minutes, and the writhing bodies on the mat did not break apart, and the explosion did not come.

When it did come, it came first in Lady Musura. Her fingernails sank deep into Blade's back, so that sharp pain penetrated even through the erotic daze that surrounded him. Her lips curled back from small white teeth, and all the breath in her body came out in a series of great whooping gasps. Blade felt her pelvic muscles twisting and contracting like bands of steel, and her wet channel tightening wildly around him.

Then his own explosion came, and for a little while he was unaware of anything around him. A dozen armed men might have entered the room, and he would not have been able to raise a finger—or even an eyebrow.

But the frenzy passed, and he sank down on top of Lady Musura, still deep within her but supporting his weight on his elbows. Silence returned to the room, silence broken only by deep gasping breaths as they both tried to refill their starved lungs.

Eventually Blade rolled off the woman and lay down on the mat beside her. Her warm limbs wrapped themselves around him again, but this time she was only making herself comfortable for sleep. The silence in the room deepened.

Blade and Lady Musura found the lovemaking neither unexpected nor unwelcome. It deepened the bond between them and took away some of the tension of waiting for Yezjaro's reply.

But the last of the tension did not disappear until that reply came, four days later. It came on a single sheet of paper, tightly folded, sealed with wax, and shoved under the door of their room.

BLADE AND LADY MUSURA

AT THE THIRD NIGHT HOUR OF THIS DAY NEXT WEEK, AT THE MIDDEN OF THE INN OF THE PERFUMED WIND ON THE STREET OF SAYA. WITH YOU WE SHALL BE TWENTY-NINE. VENGEANCE TO OUR LORD. DEATH TO LORD GERON.

YEZJARO

20

The darkness around them was thick and silent. The heavy damp air caught and held a dozen different ghastly stenches from the garbage pit across the alley. Blade's black silk mask concealed his face from prying eyes, but it couldn't keep out the smell.

No doubt that was why Yezjaro had picked this spot for the rendezvous. No one would voluntarily linger in this reeking alley, not even a Hongshu agent trying to sniff out treason. He would sniff out too many other things and depart in haste.

Footsteps sounded to the left, toward the end of the alley. Blade saw Lady Musura's eyes flicker toward him. They flattened themselves against the flaking brick wall and drew their swords. Both wore black from head to foot, and even their swords had been dulled with soot to avoid reflecting the slightest gleam of light.

The footsteps continued, coming on lightly but fast. Then a figure appeared in the alley, dimly silhouetted against the pale light at the end. It seemed to hear or see something ahead. Then it stopped and spread out black-clad arms. It raised one hand high overhead, crooking the wrist to the left. It dropped the other hand down to its waist and made a V with thumb and forefinger.

That was Yezjaro's recognition signal. Blade and Lady Musura stepped out into the alley and approached the instructor. Like them, he wore only black. All they could see were his eyes. But there was a savage gleam of triumph and anticipation in those eyes. It brightened as he shook hands with both people. Then he turned and beckoned them to follow him.

"The others are already on their way to the first point."

The "first point" was the entrance to the tunnels that led into the palace. Four men normally guarded it, four men from the households of the principal courtesans. Tonight they were four doomed men.

The three slipped through the dark streets of Deyun, swords sheathed but eyes searching constantly in all directions for any sign of spies or ambush. Blade found himself holding his breath from time to time, listening for the slightest sound. He heard only the soft patter of three sets of sandaled feet on the stones and an occasional snore or rattling shutter from the houses they passed.

What seemed like hours could only have been a few minutes. Then they were crossing a final street, with the walls and roofs of the palace at the far end, and darting into the shelter of another alley. Black-clad shapes lurked in all the corners and doorways along this alley. Yezjaro stepped forward and made his signal again. For a moment the darkness came silently alive with moving ghostly shapes. Then a more solid clump of darkness formed about halfway down the alley, in front of a high wooden gate in the wall.

There was a noble's garden beyond the wall as well as the concealed tunnel entrance with its four guards. Four guards who would have to die silently and swiftly before they could raise any sort of alarm or send any sort of warning.

Here was another call for Lady Musura's wall-climbing talents. She quickly scanned the wall up and down, searching through the darkness for hand and footholds. Then she launched herself at the bricks. Once a foot scraped harshly across flaking brick, dislodging a few bits that pattered down into the alley. Everyone froze, hands on weapons. But after a moment it was clear that no one inside had heard. The men in the alley relaxed—as much as they could—while Lady Musura continued her climb.

Then she was on top of the wall, flattening herself there and craning her neck to look down into the garden. From the alley she was visible only as a low dark hump on top of the wall, moving slowly and sinuously. Blade knew she was unslinging a short bow and nocking a silent arrow to it.

Then in a single movement she leaped to her feet and raised her bow. At the same moment Blade and Yezjaro stepped up to the gate and rapped sharply on it with their sheathed short swords. Irritable voices sounded on the other side of the gate, then they heard the clank of a massive iron latch. The gate began to slide open, moving silently in a greased wooden slot. A bearded face under a leather helmet looked sourly out at them. Then startled eyes flared white in the face, and a mouth opened to shout.

The shout never came out. With one flick of his wrist Yezjaro unsheathed the short sword. With another flick he slashed it across the man's throat. Then he lunged forward with his other hand, grabbed the man by the beard, and pulled him forward as he died. His body sagged to the ground, pumping out blood and effectively jamming the gate open.

The first man's fall revealed two more standing behind him. Blade's arm snapped up, and a spear specially shortened for throwing at close quarters flashed through the opening. It took one of the men squarely in the right eye, driving into the brain. He was dead before he struck the ground.

The third man turned to dash for the rear of the garden and the tunnel entrance. As he left the shadow of the wall, there was a faint *sssh* and a louder *thuck*! of an arrow sinking into flesh. The man gasped, threw up his hands, staggered a few paces, then fell on his face. He landed with a splash in one of the ponds. As the ripples in the pond died away, silence descended on the garden again. The remaining guard was already dead, lying sprawled across the stone slab that concealed the tunnel entrance, one of Lady Musura's arrows in his throat.

All four guards were down, without a single unusual noise to warn anybody. Lady Musura jumped down from the top of the wall, landing feather-light from ten feet up. Yezjaro dragged the first guard's body out of the opening while Blade put his shoulder to the gate and pushed it the rest of the way open.

Doifuzan emerged from the darkness of the alley and looked down at the sprawled bodies. "We are well begun," he said softly. Blade needed no reminding that these first four victims of the night would only be the first—and most likely by far the easiest.

The tunnel was much darker than the night above, and also damper, smellier, and much dirtier. In many places the roughly mortared stones dripped slime. Elsewhere they were encrusted with centuries of filth. It brushed off at the slightest touch, showering down on the twenty-nine *uroi* as they passed, powdering and caking their clothes. Blade suspected that if they hadn't already been wearing black, they would have been before they reached the far end of the tunnel.

They moved along at a swift trot, following the light from a single lantern Yezjaro carried in one hand. They moved with drawn swords, except for the six smallest *uroi*. These were enveloped from neck to ankles in the heavy green canvas cloaks the courtesans wore to protect their silk robes from the filth of the tunnels. These disguised men would be the first out of the tunnel at the end of the journey.

Blade was determined not to spend a single unnecessary minute in the tunnel. In fact, he found himself having to fight not to break from a trot into a run. Once they were loose in Lord Geron's house, it would be hard to keep them from doing a memorable night's work. But if an attack came here in the tunnel, they would be as helpless as kittens in a basket. They would die unsung and unhonored, and those few who heard the tale of the twenty-nine *uroi* of Lord Tsekuin would call it a tale of foolishly wasted lives.

In fifteen minutes they had reached the point where the tunnel branched. Blade knew they must now be well inside the walls of the Hongshu's palace. But that made no real difference. They were no less helpless against attack in the tunnel now than they had been before.

They did not halt until Yezjaro raised his lantern over his head and waved it three times. In the half-darkness ahead Blade saw a rusty iron ladder rising through the roof of the tunnel. At the base of the ladder was an iron plaque, also red with rust and green with slime. Under the rust and slime, Blade could make out the badge of Lord Geron.

Most of the twenty-nine *uroi* flattened themselves against the walls of the tunnel, letting the six disguised as courtesans move up to the front. Doifuzan came with them. He and Yezjaro would be going up the ladder first, pretending to be the guards sent from the Warm Gates quarter with this group of ladies. It was a matter of honor for Doifuzan, once the first *dabuno* of Lord Tsekuin, to be the first man into the house of Lord Geron.

Doifuzan and Yezjaro vanished upward into the darkness at the top of the ladder. The six got ready to follow them. The other *uroi* tried to make themselves silent and invisible.

Five sharp thumps from above, as Doifuzan knocked on the cover over the shaft. Five more, in a carefully spaced two-one-two pattern. That was the normal recognition signal for this month. Then a *clank* and grating, squealing noises as someone on the surface pulled the cover aside.

"Six ladies for the service of this house," said Yezjaro.

"What's this? Six ladies from the Warm Gates? We didn't have any ordered for tonight. It was next week that–"

"You didn't? Then why did we get clear instructions to deliver them here?"

"I don't know. Somebody made a mistake, I guess. But–"

"You're damned right somebody made a mistake. And we're going to find out who." Clatterings as Yezjaro climbed the rest of the way up to the surface.

"Wait a minute! You can't come up into the house if you're not–!"

"The devil we can't, my friend! I'm not going to keep the ladies down in that stinking hole while you people wake up your superiors and argue."

Lady Musura took the cue. Her voice was shrill with proptest and indignation, a perfect imitation of a high-priced, tempermental courtesan. "What in Kunkoi's name is going on up there, you fools? If we have to wait here much longer, half of us will fall ill. And none from the Warm Gates will ever come again to the house of Lord Geron!"

That last threat did the job. None of the guards wanted to be the one responsible for such a disaster.

Blade heard the grumbling and muttering of several confused men talking together, then:

"All right, bring them on up. They can wait out here, though."

"Very well. Come on up, ladies."

The disguised *uroi* scrambled up the ladder, one by one. Blade and Lady Musura stationed themselves one on each side of the ladder and waited, listening.

They heard the "ladies" climb out, one by one, and Doifuzan's voice counting them off, also one by one. "That is all of them."

Those words were the signal. From the darkness above came a quick series of soft but deadly noises. Swords being drawn, then sheathed again in human bodies. Blood gurgling in the throats of dying men. The thump of bodies falling on soft earth and the crackle as they fell into bushes. A half-choked cry, cut off brutally by a hand clamped over someone's mouth. Scrabbling footsteps—and then a body came hurtling down from the darkness above, to land with a *sqump*! on the slimy stones at Blade's feet. The man's eyes had rolled up in his head, showing only the whites, and blood was still pumping from a slash under his ribcage. Lady Musura brought her foot down hard on the man's throat. Cartilage crackled and the man heaved and writhed in a final convulsion, then lay still.

"Time to come up," came Doifuzan's voice from above.

Blade went up the ladder like a cork from a champagne bottle, hardly feeling the iron rungs under his feet. He vaulted out of the shaft and stood with his sword drawn as the rest of the party swarmed up the shaft after him.

Three guards lay dead or dying around the entrance to the shaft. They were apparently all to die in silence. At least the house that loomed beyond the trees at the far end of the garden remained silent and almost dark.

But the alarm would be given sooner or later. Now they had to move faster than ever, storming through a house they did not know, sealing off all escape routes and then combing it room by room and nook by cranny. Speed, speed, speed! If anything could doom Lord Geron, it would be speed!

The six disguised *uroi* finished stripping off their disguises. Doifuzan looked around, and Blade could see his lips move as he counted off the twenty-eight fighters standing in the darkness around him. So far all the dead had been the enemy's. That wouldn't last much longer, however much luck they had.

Doifuzan raised his hand. Yezjaro threw the lantern down on the ground. It flickered and died. The instructor's voice rang out in the darkness, roaring out defiance to any ears that might be listening.

"Thus shall Lord Geron also go down into the darkness. Those who served Lord Tsekuin—follow me!"

They dashed toward the house, spreading out as they ran. They crashed through bushes and pounded across small bridges, making what seemed to Blade more noise than a herd of stampeding cattle. Before Doifuzan had reached the door, shouts came from inside. Then women started screaming and lights began to flicker behind windows.

Doifuzan was the first to reach the door, Yezjaro close behind him. Just as Blade reached the house, someone lit a lantern inside, almost in front of him. He saw two silhouettes dark against the yellow white oiled paper of the window. Reflexes took over. His spear shot forward, stabbing through the heavy paper with a sharp *pop* and skewering the left-hand figure just above the waist. Fortunately the howl of surprise and agony was a man's. The other silhouette vanished, as blood from the dying man sprayed dark against the window.

Blade drew his sword and hacked a broad triangular opening in the paper. Several men ran up as he did so, and dove through the opening as he stepped back. After that came Lady Musura, both swords drawn, leaping like a gazelle through the window in a single ten-foot bound. Only after that could Blade enter the house.

As his feet hit the mats inside, he heard a smashing and splintering of wood as the door toppled inward. Several of Lord Geron's household *dabuni* sprang back in front of it. One didn't move fast enough. The falling door caught him and slammed him to the floor. He screamed once, then life and breath went out of him in a gasp as Doifuzan and a dozen attackers came trampling across the door and his body.

The dozen took the little cluster of defenders head-on, crashing into them like a tidal wave. Noise exploded through the room as both sides swung fast and furiously. The defenders were too surprised and too badly outnumbered to think of tactics. The attackers were in too much of a hurry.

So there was no maneuvering for position, no complicated footwork, none of the delicate style common in Gaikon swordfighting. Doifuzan himself led the attackers, chopping downward with his sword as crudely and brutally as a butcher beheading a pig. But his stroke smashed down an enemy's guard and bit through the man's collarbone and ribs into his heart.

Some of the other attackers weren't so lucky. Two went down from crude slashes and cuts, writhing on the floor under their comrades' feet, howling and screaming. But four men had no chance against ten who could get around their flanks. Swords fell, then rose red and dripping. The smell of blood filled the room. Then the four defenders were down on the bloody mats, along with another of the attackers. Seven men dead, in less than a minute.

Doifuzan led the survivors off deeper into the house at a dead run. Some of the *dabuni* who had come in through the window started off after them. All of the attackers were shouting and yelling loudly enough to wake anyone still sleeping in the house.

Blade grabbed one of the *dabuni* by the collar as he was about to dash off and bellowed in his ear, "Follow me, in Kunkoi's name! We've got to spread out!" He waved a hand off to the right, where a hall led away into the shadows.

As if Blade's gesture had conjured them out of the floor, six armed men appeared in the hall, pounding toward Blade at a dead run. One was carrying a bow. He shot, and the arrow sank deep into the thigh of the *dabuno* beside Blade. The man gasped, reached down, jerked the arrow out, threw it to the floor, then clamped a hand tightly over the spurting wound. Sword raised, he staggered toward the oncoming men.

Another arrow sank into his stomach. But as the first enemy came within reach, his sword flashed through a deadly arc. The first man's head wobbled on its shoulders, then thumped to the floor. The headless body drove on for a few steps more until it collided with the dying *dabuno*. Both went down, neither got up.

Before they hit the floor, Blade hurled his spear at the archer. It drove into his chest just below the breastbone. The impact at close range nearly knocked the man off his feet. He staggered, then swung around in a circle. The jutting shaft of the spear got in the way of one of his comrades. As he ducked under it, he was for a moment wide open. That moment was all that Blade needed to step forward and bring his sword down. Steel bit through bone and flesh again, and another headless body hit the floor. Then Blade had to leap back as the three surviving enemies came on.

For a moment things looked bad. He was one against three, and he had only his sword. But the three men had just seen three of their comrades die in less than a minute. No loyalty to Lord Geron could give them the courage to approach Blade too closely. He found it easy to guard against their cautious strokes. But he began to wonder how long this might go on. If more defenders appeared, to take him in the rear . . .

He had barely finished the thought when he heard something swish through the air. Then a *jinai's* throwing dart blossomed in the right eye of the center man. He squalled like a wounded panther and plunged forward. On the fringes of his field of vision Blade saw a slim black-clad figure bounding forward to meet the *dabuno*. Lady Musura dove to come in low, the *dabuno* seemed to fly into the air, then both crashed to the floor and rolled over and over. They struck against the wall with a crash and Lady Musura bounced to her feet. The *dabuno* kicked twice and lay still.

Blade flashed a silent smile of greeting to the woman, and turned back to his two remaining opponents. Before he had finished the turn there was only one, as Lady Musura cut in to the left and took out the *dabuno* there. A quick dart under his sword, a kick to his kneecap, and a knife thrust up under his chin until the point went into his brain—then there was another corpse on the floor.

Blade fended off a cut from his last opponent and smiled again.

"Leave this one for me."

He saw her nod and step aside to keep a watch

down the hall, then he turned his full attention to his opponent. They had room for footwork now, and they went around in a circle three times. Then the *dabuno* attacked. Blade held his ground, beat the other's sword upward and away from his head, then drove in with a cut that hacked through the other's left arm at a single blow. As the man shifted his sword to his right hand and tried to come at Blade again, Blade's own sword darted first right, then left. As it darted right it smashed the man's sword out of his hand. As it swung left it slashed across the throat, half-severing his head. The dying man fell across his own sword. Blade and Lady Musura stepped over the body and headed down the hall.

After a moment Blade remembered to look behind him and see if anyone was following them to guard their rear and if necessary their line of retreat. No one was. He did not stop—there was not time for that. But he swore to himself. Damn those hotheads! They were dashing off as the impulse took them, everybody too bloodthirsty and eager to think clearly. Even Doifuzan didn't seem to care about making sure the house was thoroughly searched and all exits guarded. That was going to leave him and Lady Musura with too damned much work for any two people to handle. But there wasn't anything they could do about it.

They moved on down the hall, checking each room as they passed. A few yards farther on they came to a wide flight of stairs. There seemed to be another, more brightly lit hall at the top. Blade nodded toward the stairs and Lady Musura followed him up. He couldn't help thinking that this was a bloody good way to be ambushed or killed by mistake by your own side, let alone by the enemy! But the second floor had to be cleared, and it looked as though the job was going to be up to them.

The hallway at the top seemed deserted. But Blade

wasn't taking any chances. He kicked down the door of each room as he came to it, while Lady Musura covered his back and kept an eye on the hall in both directions.

He found no one, armed or unarmed, alive or dead, in any of the rooms. Some of them must have been living quarters—their floors were covered with sleeping mats. Overturned cups and bottles, scattered sandals, and tumbled blankets showed where some of the rooms had been hastily evacuated.

The thick wooden floor muffled the sounds of the battle that still seemed to be raging below. Blade was beginning to worry. Was everybody in such a blind fury that nobody was going to think of the second floor? That might give Lord Geron a good chance to escape.

They came to a bend where the hall turned at right angles to the left. Thirty feet farther on it came to a dead end. The walls on either side were bare plastered wood, and the floor underfoot was unpolished and scarred. About halfway to the blank end of the hall was a small door in the left-hand wall.

Blade scanned the empty hall so thoroughly that he would have spotted a cockroach if there had been one crawling across the ceiling. He didn't like the silence in this isolated hall. It was unnatural in the middle of a battle. If someone was lying in ambush in that side room . . .

Then he noticed that there was a faint line at the edge of one of the panels at the far end of the hall. A dark line for most of its length. But about halfway up Blade saw a faint, flickering yellow glow seeping through the crack.

Silently he took Lady Musura by the shoulder with one hand and pointed with the other. She nodded. Then he pointed at the side door. She nodded again and stepped cat-footed down the hall, stalking along until she was directly opposite the door. When she was in position, Blade made his slow, careful way down the last stretch of hall. He felt sweat trickling down his back as he passed the door, and he wished for the hundredth time that he had eyes in the back of his head. By the time he was ten feet from the end of the hall, there was no mistaking it. A light was burning in some concealed compartment behind that panel. Then he was only five feet away—and the lamp went out.

As it did, the door Lady Musura was watching flew open and the room behind it spewed fighting men into the hall. Lady Musura sprang forward. Blade's mouth opened in a shout as he realized she would never survive, wading into a fight against such odds at close quarters.

She was moving fast as she crashed into the five men who were already out in the hall, her swords reaching out to either side. Blade saw the point of her long sword go in under one man's chin, her short sword drive downward into another's groin—and a third man's spear take her in the chest. The point drove into her right breast and came out between her shoulder blades. Her body arched, but one leg shot up and a foot took the spearman in the groin. He howled and staggered, letting go his grip on the spear. Lady Musura slashed him in the back with her long sword. Then a fourth man struck downward, laying her thigh open to the bone. She fell on her back, writhing as the spear twisted itself about inside her.

The forth man had about three seconds to savor his victory. Then Blade's sword split his skull from crown to chin and he collapsed on top of Lady Musura. The fifth man was vanishing down the hall already. Blade turned, saw more *dabuni* crowding out of the room, and attacked.

It would have been safer for him to stay out in the hall and take the men as they came out, no more than one or two at a time. It would have been safer, but it wouldn't have matched his mood. He was not a cold-blooded professional now, he was a killing machine in a white-hot rage. He sprang through the doorway, landing on the shaft of a spear thrust toward him. The shock pulled the spearman forward. Blade's short sword jabbed up into the man's throat as he toppled down onto it. The man thudded to the floor, jerking the short sword out of Blade's hand. Blade leaped clear of the corpse rolling at his feet and slashed at a man to his right. Flesh and ribs split under Blade's sword and the man crashed backward against the wall, knocking over a lamp. It broke, spilling burning oil down the side of a large crate and onto the mats. The oil also ran onto the fallen man's face. His screams drowned out the crackling of the flames as they ran across the mats and began to climb the wall.

Those were the last details Blade remembered for a while. Not a very long while—no more than a minute or two. But it didn't take very long for a man in Blade's mood to kill six more men with a Gaikon sword.

When Blade's head cleared, he realized that the room was filled with smoke and that a good part of the floor matting and one wall were on fire. Eight bodies lay around him in a semicircle, all gashed or gutted or missing arms, legs, or heads. His sword was red and slippery with blood from point to hilt, and so was his sword arm.

He backed hastily out into the hall. As he did so, he heard a noise to his left. He whirled and saw someone in a dirty brown robe struggling with the panel at the end of the hall. Whoever it was was obviously trying to get back into the compartment that lay behind the panel.

Blade knew he couldn't cover the distance before the panel closed on the man. But at his feet sprawled the bodies of Lady Musura's victims. Blade bent, grabbed one by an ankle, and swung him hard and high. At exactly the right moment he let go. The body sailed through the air and crashed into the brown-robed man, smashing him against the panel and knocking his legs out from under him. Half-stunned, the man rolled on the floor, trying to fumble a knife out of his sash. Blade charged down the hall, kicked the knife out of the man's hand, then grabbed him by the collar and jerked him to his feet. A thin, dark face, the right side covered with half-healed red scars, stared at Blade. The eyes widened in appalled recognition, and the mouth opened to scream.

It was Lord Geron.

Blade shoved the Hongshu's second chancellor back against the wall as hard as he could. The bare skull smashed into the wood and Lord Geron slumped down, unconscious. With his prisoner immobilized for the time being, Blade turned to Lady Musura.

She was dead—must have been dead for several minutes now. Her contorted, bloodless face and sightless eyes stared upward at Blade. He bent down and gently pressed the eyelids closed.

There was a knife in her hand, and Blade knew what she must have been planning to do with it. When the *jinai* died, they often tried to slash their faces so that no one would recognize them. But it did not matter now whether or not anyone recognized Lady Musura. She had died with her face intact, and Blade found himself glad of that. She had found very little joy in a life of hard service, with a hard death at the end of it.

The quick footsteps of a number of men sounded on the stairs. Again Blade spun around, to see

Doifuzan, Yezjaro, and five or six others trot around the bend in the hall. They stopped as they saw Blade standing over Lady Musura, the bodies around him, and the smoke billowing out of the room. Then Yezjaro's eyes traveled beyond Blade—and widened in delighted astonishment as they fell on Lord Geron. The instructor looked at Doifuzan.

"I concede the honor to you, First *Dabuno*."

Doifuzan shook his head. "I think both of us should concede it to Blade. Without his aid, it might have taken us five long years or more to bring our plans to completion. He found a way for us here. And it seems to have been his skill and his sword that in the end took the man we sought. Blade, I doubt if we shall live long enough to do you the honor you deserve. But we can at least do this."

"Indeed, you speak the truth. Blade, the honor of striking down Lord Geron shall be yours."

Blade bowed mechanically, turned, and drew his sword. The battle-fury had left him and he felt drained, half-sick, and he wished only to get the business over with. Lord Geron was still unconscious when Blade's sword slashed down through his scrawny neck, and his head rolled across the floor.

"I hope he knew who was in his house, and why," said Doifuzan as he bent to pick up the head and place it in a linen sack.

Blade smiled grimly. "He recognized me, I know."

"Good. Then he has enough knowledge to take with him to Kunkoi." Doifuzan finished tying the neck of the sack and stood up. "I think we would do well to leave here at once. The Hongshu's soldiers may enter the garden at any time, and the house itself seems doomed." A crash from within the storeroom punctuated his remarks. The crackle and boom of the flames became fiercer, and the yellow brown smoke rolled more thickly out into the hall.

"Come, brothers. Let us be off." Doifuzan turned and led them away down the hall toward the stairs.

21

Nineteen of the twenty-nine *uroi* got safely out of the burning house, back through the tunnel, away from the Hongshu's palace. By the time they had reached the street, the fire was visible for miles. Flames shot a hundred feet into the air and lit up the base of a cloud of smoke that rose many times higher.

The streets began to come alive with people running out to stare at the fire, loudly wondering what it could mean. No one bothered the nineteen *uroi* as they tramped along, or failed to give them a clear path. In their black clothes they looked much like a party of the Hongshu's *jinai* on an urgent mission. No sensible private citizen and few soldiers would ask nineteen *jinai* their business or try to stop them. By dawn they were well outside the city, heading across country as fast as their legs would carry them, toward the emperor's precinct.

"That's a good three days' march," Yezjaro told Blade in one of their brief pauses. "But we're going to do it in two. Not on the roads, either. Until we can place ourselves under the emperor's protection, the less anybody sees of us, the better. Once the emperor has rendered his judgment on us, even the Hongshu will stand aside. Until then the Hongshu will do as he sees fit. Need I bore you with details?" The instructor was haggard and filthy, and there were hollow circles under eyes reddened by fatigue and smoke. But he held onto a good deal of his sword-sharp wit.

Blade shook his head. "No, I think not. I doubt that the Hongshu will thank us for this past night's work."

"Nor, I fear, will the emperor," said Yezjaro. "At least he will not dare to do so openly. And what that may lead to—I have my doubts. But let us leave my suspicions where they are for the present, and march."

They marched. They marched as Blade had never done during his military service in home dimension, nor in any land or among any people in Dimension X. They stopped once for a few hours to sleep, and twice to eat and drink in small inns huddled at the edges of lonely forests. Otherwise they tramped steadily along, up hills, down into valleys, across brief stretches of lowlands and paddy fields, along paths winding through dark insect-ridden forests. Blade lost track of time, almost lost track of night and day and the passing landscape. His legs were white-hot pillars of fire, his throat a mass of dry gravel, his eyes glowing coals. But he kept on going because the others were, although few of them seemed in much better shape than he was.

On the morning of the third day they came to the crest of the last hill. Beyond the forest that spread across the valley below Blade saw castle towers with gold and orange banners streaming from them.

"The emperor's precinct," said Yezjaro. There was relief in his voice, but also something else. Call it—well, acceptance. Acceptance of whatever might be waiting for them on the other side of the forest. Blade began to suspect that there were problems yet to come that he wasn't being told about. He was tempted to say so bluntly. But before he could speak, a dozen riders burst out of the forest below and began mounting the slope toward the *uroi* on top.

Blade's hand went to his sword hilt, then he saw that one of the horsemen was carrying the same orange and gold banner that flew over the castle. An imperial welcoming party? In any case, not the Hong-shu's men. Blade started to relax, then he saw the tension still written all over Yezjaro's face. So instead he drew himself up as straight as his exhaustion and aching muscles permitted. There was an impressive dignity in the way the other men were standing, ready to accept the emperor's welcome whatever it might be. Blade did his best to match it. He kept his face expressionless and waited.

The horsemen appeared to be picking their way more cautiously as the slope steepened under them. Then, suddenly, Doifuzan stiffened like a puppet pulled upright by its strings. Pulling his sheathed swords from his sash, he dropped them on the grass. Then he knelt, head bowed. Before he had completed the movements, Yezjaro was following him, as were all the other *dabuni*.

Blade's bewilderment must have been written all over his face, because Yezjaro turned his head slightly and half-whispered, "The high prince himself rides to greet us. It is seldom that the emperor's own eldest son and heir comes forth. This is a mighty moment."

"But not necessarily a fortunate one for us?" Blade could not help asking the question as he joined the others on his knees.

Yezjaro was silent for a moment before nodding. "You still see clearly, Blade."

"I see what is on your face, my friend. And what is on your face is not—"

Yezjaro put a finger to his lips. Blade nodded and turned to look at the high prince, who had now moved out ahead of the other horsemen.

The high prince could not be more than seventeen, but he sat his horse like a cavalryman. He wore a short tunic that left muscular arms half-bare, and his tanned face showed no trace of youthful softness or baby fat. He wore a gilded breastplate and greaves, and a leather helmet with brass cheekpieces and an orange feather crest.

The high prince's father was an indecisive scholar, or so they said. But the high prince himself was a warrior. If he wasn't, Blade knew that he had lost the ability to recognize a warrior when he saw one.

The high prince's horse reared as it reached the top of the slope. The rider gentled it, then flung himself out of the saddle with an athlete's grace and swiftness and a complete lack of ceremoniousness. His companions reined in their horses and dismounted more carefully.

The high prince crossed his arms on his chest and said in a clear but high-pitched voice, "Welcome, *uroi*, in the emperor's name and in mine as well. I grant that here and now you may raise your eyes and look upon me."

There were gasps of surprise from the *uroi*, then slowly, one by one, their exhausted grimy faces rose to look upon their future ruler. The high prince waited until he had the attention of all of them, then continued.

"You come from taking your vengeance upon Lord Geron for his betrayal of Lord Tsekuin. Is that not so, Doifuzan?"

"It is so, Exalted One."

"You bear his head?"

"We do." Doifuzan motioned to the *uroi* who had been carrying the sack. The man ran forward to kneel before the high prince and place the sack on the grass at the high prince's feet.

"Word has spread swiftly, as swiftly as birds upon the wind. The deed of the *uroi* who once served Lord Tsekuin already stands in Gaikon like high mountains. May Kunkoi grant that it stands as long as the mountains, as an example to men who come after us."

"We are not worthy of such fame, Exal—"

"That is not for you to judge, Doifuzan." Then the high prince fell silent. Even in his fatigue, Blade's trained ear told him that the young man was hesitating. He has praised us highly, thought Blade. If he is hesitating over what comes next, it's probably bad news.

"However—" began the high prince, and stopped again. That settles it, thought Blade. I've never heard anyone begin a sentence that wasn't bad news with "However."

"However," and now the words came out in a rush, "you have in your honorable vengeance slain a servant of the Hongshu, the Strong Younger Brother, whose hand is spread over Gaikon to keep the peace within it." And to grab whatever his greedy heart desires, added Blade to himself. He nearly said it out loud.

"Therefore, it is fit and proper that your deaths shall follow." Blade tensed. "It is the will of the emperor that you shall join Lord Tsekuin by that same honorable road which he used, and before the sun sets tomorrow. This honor is yours and none shall impair it in any way. For the emperor, it is spoken."

The high prince worked his mouth for a moment, perhaps trying to get a bad taste out of it. Then he vaulted into the saddle and spurred his horse away down the hill, as though he could no longer face the men he had condemned to death.

That was certainly what he had done. Blade turned it over and over in his mind and could come up with no other answer. Before sunset tomorrow, they would all be dead by ritual suicide.

The high prince had called it an honor. Blade

looked at the other eighteen men, and the relief and even joy on their faces. He realized that it might indeed be an honor. At least by the standards of Gaikon. But—were there other standards for him to follow, here and now?

If he could even think of that question, it would be a hard one to answer. He had the feeling that tonight was going to be full of grim, lonely thinking.

The *uroi* were quartered in an empty barracks in the military camp to the south of the palace. The servants who waited on them were willing to meet their every want. But those wants were few. Some of the *uroi* felt they should spend this last night fasting and praying. Those who were less strict still had little appetite for the food set before them. Not even Yezjaro was interested in the wine and the women they could have had. Some of the *uroi* were simply too tired to think about anything except a good night's sleep.

So no one bothered Blade when he went out after dark to sit under a tree and consider what he should do. He had expected to find his decision brutally hard to make. But that was not what happened.

None of the *uroi* were going to try to escape. That was obvious. They had done everything they had been living for when Lord Geron's head fell to the floor of his burning house. If they had then joined their ten comrades who were now ashes in the ruins of that house, it would have made no difference to them. Men who felt their lives were over would not disobey an order of their emperor. They had refused to strike at the Hongshu when they had the best of reasons for doing so. They would not defy the emperor when they had no reason except saving their own skins. None of them would. Not even Yezjaro, the cheerful, pleasure-loving young instructor, would try to gain the many years of life he should have ahead of him by defying the emperor.

So if he fled, Blade knew he would flee alone.

He probably wouldn't have much trouble getting away from the emperor's precinct and surviving in the woods until he was called back to home dimension. He saw no signs that the *uroi* were being particularly well guarded. If he picked up his weapons now and strode away into the darkness, it would be easy to leave certain death behind him.

But he would also be leaving behind him eighteen doomed men, who had accepted their doom. Eighteen men who had fought as his comrades in a deadly battle to do their duty, who had in the end accepted him and honored him as first among them. They would call him a coward. If he lived, he would have to live with the knowledge that they had died thinking this of him.

And what would his flight do to the example the *uroi* wanted to set? The high prince's words had been clear. The servants had made it even clearer. The twenty-nine *uroi* would go into the legends of Gaikon as men who had stood faithful to their lord to death.

But what would happen to the legend if one of them fled at the last minute? Particularly if the one who fled was the one who had made their swift vengeance possible? Would the flight of that one man diminish what the other twenty-eight had done? Blade knew the codes and standards of Gaikon too well to doubt it. The tale would be flawed and the memory of those who had been his comrades diminished.

Perhaps it was a silly notion. In fact he was quite sure it was, looked at soberly. But nonetheless he did not want to take anything away from the legend that the twenty-nine *uroi* had begun. If that meant accepting Gaikon's standards and the death they would bring—well, so be it.

And there was more. The present emperor might be too weak to inspire people to resist the Hongshu. But the high prince was a warrior, and if he lived to mount his father's throne Gaikon would have an emperor who might want to rule as well as reign.

If that happened, the Hongshu would have a mighty rival. Those who hated the Hongshu would have a rallying point. And the legend of the twenty-nine *uroi* would be part of that rallying. To weaken the legend might be to reduce the chances of bringing to an end the Hongshu's tyranny. Blade had risked his life in a dozen strange worlds to help their people in one way or another. What was different about accepting an honorable death here in Gaikon, if it would help strike at the Hongshu?

Nothing.

With that settled in his own mind, Blade found it easy to return to the barracks and go peacefully to sleep.

Lord Tsekuin had knelt to die on white sand. The *uroi* who had avenged him knelt to die on green grass, beyond the forest to the west of the emperor's precinct. But like their lord, each knelt on a small square of black silk. Each wore white, with a red sash. Blade had shoved under his sash the pouch with the diamond, and had put Lady Musura's short sword on the ground in front of him. That would be his death-weapon. It was a last honor that he could do her.

In the center of the circle stood a tall pole. From its top Lord Tsekuin's banner floated out on the evening breeze. A banner proscribed and banned by the Hongshu—but not by the emperor. Or rather, not by the high prince. It was no secret that he had watched the setting up of the pole, and then raised Lord Tsekuin's banner with his own hands.

No, the high prince was being open about what he thought of the Hongshu and the Hongshu's ways of ruling. Was he perhaps trying to spark rebellion even now? Blade couldn't help wondering. But it was idle wondering. Whatever the high prince might be planning didn't make much difference to him. In barely ten minutes he would be either dead or back in home dimension. More likely dead.

The moment of death for the nineteen *uroi* was fixed for sunset exactly. Blade looked toward the west, where a swollen orange ball seemed to hang in a luminous sky just above spiky black tree-tops. Less than ten minutes—quite a bit less, he suspected. A few minutes more or less didn't matter, in any case. They would make no difference in the astronomical odds against his living to return to home dimension.

Blade had often wondered what would pass through his mind in the last minutes before his death. But now he realized that all his previous imaginings had been meaningless. He was not going to die in the heat of furious action, brought down by great odds or bad luck. Nor was he going to die in bed of old age or illness. In his profession the second had never been very likely. But he had always accepted that as the only other prospect.

He had never imagined that he would be as he was now, sitting and calmly waiting for the signal to die by his own hand.

Calmly? Yes, calmly. He had accepted that there was no alternative that would permit him to live comfortably with himself—or avoid doing harm here in Gaikon. With this acceptance had come a calmness that seemed likely to last until he had no more need for any emotion of any sort.

The sun sank down. Blade felt sweat trickling down the back of his neck. The breeze seemed to be dying away. He could no longer feel it on his skin, and the tops of the trees were no longer bending toward him. They stood motionless against the sunset sky, with the great wavering ball of the sun sinking down toward them—

—and touching them.

A trumpet sounded from far away over the trees, from the palace itself. The boom of several massive gongs being slowly beaten followed. Yezjaro raised his head, and his dark eyes stared into Blade's. Blade stared back, and met Doifuzan's stare as well. One hand moved to open his tunic, while the other picked up the short sword lying on the grass in front of him.

All around the circle, the others did the same.

Blade unsheathed the short sword and held it out in front of him, its point toward his abdomen.

Again, eighteen *uroi* did the same.

Then, just before Blade could tense his muscles to drive the sword in, pain flared—suddenly, savagely—in his head. Sweat sprang out on his face and hands, and he had to clamp his mouth shut hard to keep from gasping out loud. He did not want to make any sound that would give his comrades the impression that he was losing his nerve.

But hope was also flaring in him, even more intense than the pain. The computer was calling him, calling him back to home dimension. He was going to make it home! And without dishonor or disgrace. If he simply vanished . . .

Then the pain faded, and so did the hope. Blade realized that he might make it home. But he also might still die here in Gaikon. He could not delay his blow much longer. If he did, he would do much of the damage he had feared, whether he died in the end or not.

No, it was time to do what had to be done. With a convulsive snap of his wrist, he drove the short sword in.

It struck so hard that the shock kept him from feeling any pain for a moment. Then as the pain struck, before he could start drawing the sword across, his head seemed to explode. His hand dropped away from the sword hilt because he had lost the strength to hold on. Hope rose in him again. With it rose the fear that the soldier standing behind him with a sword might swing prematurely.

It would be a bloody odd situation if he returned to home dimension in two pieces, or as a headless corpse!

The twilight seemed to turn to a shimmering green. Blade looked down, saw the sword in his hand flickering and glowing with raw red and golden hues. Across the circle he saw Yezjaro, bending over as he drew the sword across his stomach. But the instructor's eyes were fixed on Blade, and his face showed more surprise than pain.

A *swish*, and Blade saw a sword whistling past. He realized that the soldier behind must have swung to behead him. But he was no longer a solid object to those in Gaikon—or their weapons. Soon they would be gone, and he would be home.

The greenness was darkening now. Pain roared again in Blade's head, and he found it hard to keep his eyes open. But Yezjaro was still looking at him, and at last the instructor smiled. In a voice distorted by pain and Blade's fading hearing, he shouted:

"Go in honor, Blade. Go, for Kunkoi has called you first before us all, that you may speak for us."

Then the instructor started to crumple forward. He could no longer keep agony from twisting his face. The sword of the soldier standing behind him flashed high, then swept down.

The flash of that sword was the last thing Blade saw in Gaikon. The green faded into a blackness and Blade sank down into that blackness, losing awareness of his pain, his body, everything.

22

"—glad I didn't betray the people in Gaikon. But I must say I'm glad to be back, though. Very damned glad."

Richard Blade's voice faded away into silence. Lord Leighton reached over and shut off the tape recorder. The *click* of the switch seemed to J to echo through the little room like a gunshot. He leaned back in the leather armchair, frowned, and took a firm grip on his whiskey and soda.

"Well, J," said Lord Leighton into the silence. "What do you make of that?"

"What precisely do you mean?" asked J. He used his best upper-Establishment senior civil servant's voice to conceal his own private doubts and uncertainties.

"Isn't it obvious? It seems to me that Richard was completely—sucked into—the patterns of thought in Gaikon. He was about to commit *hara-kiri* when we brought him back, damn it!"

"*Seppuku,*" said J, absently.

"Eh?"

"*Seppuku* is the more formal name for Japanese style ritual suicide. *Hara-kiri* is a rather vulgar colloquial term. It roughly translates as 'belly slitting.'"

"I see," said Lord Leighton. But it was obvious that his mind was not on the correct terminology for what

Blade had so so nearly done. After a moment's silence he continued.

"J, you've known Richard a good deal longer than anybody else with the project."

"I have."

"Speaking frankly—should we call in the psychiatrists on this one? Does what Richard did indicate that his mind's started to go?"

There it was, out in the open. The painful but unavoidable question that J had been asking himself ever since he heard what had happened to Blade in Gaikon. Fortunately, he had been considering it long enough so that he had come up with some sort of an answer. It didn't entirely satisfy him, but he was damned if he could think of a better one. If Lord Leighton could, more power to him—as long as it didn't involve throwing Richard to the headshrinkers!

"Remember the first trips to Dimension X?" J began. "Richard very nearly forgot that he *had* a home dimension existence while he was in Dimension X. He was disoriented for some time after coming back. He got over that, however, and he certainly shows no signs of it this time. Does he?"

"No. He seems perfectly normal except for—"

"That may not be a sign of abnormality. In fact, I'm fairly sure it isn't."

"So?" said Lord Leighton, testily. He did not like being disagreed with or interrupted. J was one of the few people from whom he would tolerate either.

"So consider what an enormous capacity for *loyalty* Richard has. Loyalty to England, first of all. That's what kept him going for all these trips—that and his love of adventure. For England he'll risk his life again and again and face the prospect of eventually losing it."

"Yes. But risking his life is one thing. Deliberately sitting down to kill himself seems to me to be another matter entirely. It argues something odd going on in his mind."

"Not necessarily. I think it's that same capacity for loyalty, showing itself in a new way. He's always been willing to do something to help the people of the dimension where he goes. Most of the time he's succeeded. It was the same thing this time. He realized he couldn't avoid doing damage in Gaikon—specifically, damage to the *uroi* who had fought beside him—unless he did what their standards of duty called for him to do."

"Um," said Leighton, meditatively. He seemed, if not convinced, at least not openly skeptical. "But why should Richard accept their standards?"

"The people in Gaikon lived by them, and couldn't imagine any others. Richard knew that he couldn't expect them to change, so he decided to accept what they were asking him to do. He's always been very good at understanding what other people want and need. I doubt if he'd have survived as a secret agent as long as he did without that gift. I'm *damned* sure he couldn't have survived in Dimension X without it."

Lord Leighton nodded, and his face showed understanding for the first time. "In other words, Richard Blade is a magnificently adaptable man. We sent him to Gaikon—and he adapted."

J laughed. "You've got it in a nutshell."

Leighton sighed. "Very well. I suppose we can dispense with throwing Richard to the psychiatrists over this. But I devoutly hope he doesn't have to adapt to this sort of thing very often."

"I couldn't agree with you more," said J.